# Amelia Bedelia

## Cleans Up

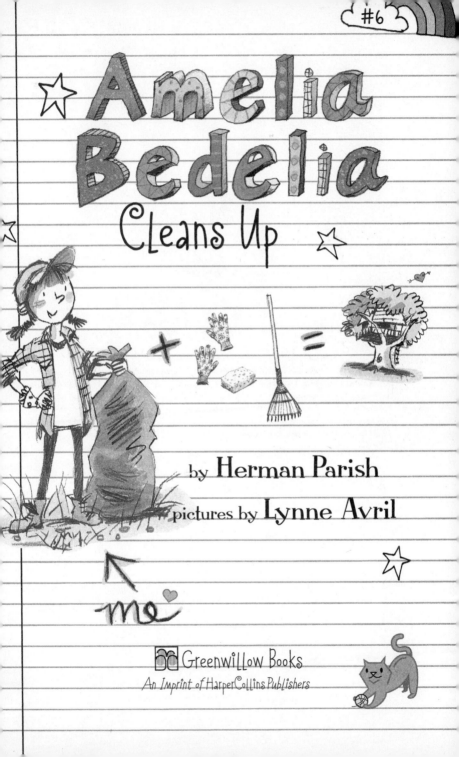

#6

# Amelia Bedelia
## Cleans Up

by Herman Parish

pictures by Lynne Avril

me

Greenwillow Books
*An Imprint of HarperCollins Publishers*

Gouache and black pencil were used to prepare the black-and-white art.

Amelia Bedelia is a registered trademark of Peppermint Partners, LLC.

The Library of Congress has cataloged an earlier printing of this title as follows:

Parish, Herman.

Amelia Bedelia cleans up / by Herman Parish ; pictures by Lynne Avril.

pages cm—(Amelia Bedelia ; #6)

Summary: "Amelia Bedelia and her friends clean up a vacant lot and build a clubhouse—with surprising results! Includes a guide to idioms used in the book and features black-and-white art throughout"—Provided by publisher.

ISBN 978-0-06-233401-5 (hardback)—ISBN 978-0-06-233400-8 (pbk. ed.)—ISBN 978-0-06-233403-9 (pob)

[1. Clubs—Fiction. 2. Friendship—Fiction. 3. Tree houses—Fiction. 4. Clubhouses—Fiction. 5. Parks—Fiction. 6. Humorous stories.] I. Title.   PZ7.P2185Aobg 2015  [E]—dc23  2014032539

15 16 17 18 19 CG/RRDH 10 9 8 7 6 5 4 3 2 1

ISBN 978-0-06-240368-1 (Amelia Bedelia Bindup #5 and #6)

Greenwillow Books, *An Imprint of* HarperCollins*Publishers*

Ages 6–10. Cover art © 2014, 2015 by Lynne Avril. Cover design by Sylvie Le Floc'h.

Also available as an ebook. www.ameliabedeliabooks.com

For Dr. Gupta and Dr. Roychowdhury—

thanks a "lot"! —H. P.


For My parents—thank you! —L. A.

# Contents

## Chapter 1

# Breezy? Yes. Easy? No . . .

Amelia Bedelia was as free as a bird. She was pedaling her bike as fast as she could. The wind was blowing in her face and blowing her hair straight back. Now she understood why Finally, her dog, loved to hang her head out the car window on trips.

Amelia Bedelia really wished that every day was this

♥ 1 ♥

WOOF! WOOF! WOOF! WOOF!

easy and breezy. Today she was riding all over town with her friends Holly and Heather. They zipped through the park, zooming past babies in strollers and woofing at the dogs out for a walk. The dogs woofed right back.

"Let's go this way!" shouted Holly.

"Follow me!" yelled Heather.

Amelia Bedelia raced after her friends. As she rode, she imagined changing her

name to Amelia Breezelia, Club President!

She had been the president for about ten minutes. Most clubs come with leaders and followers, with a bunch of rules and regulations. But this club was so new that it didn't even have a name. It had been born in Amelia Bedelia's backyard when Holly and Heather had stopped by an hour earlier.

"I'm bored," Holly had said.

"Me too," said Heather.

"We've got bikes," said Amelia Bedelia. "Let's go exploring. We can start an explorers' club!"

"Not just exploring," said Heather. "Let's have adventures."

"Let's make it our job to have adventures," said Holly.

3

"Let's start the Explorers' Adventure Club," said Heather.

"How about the Adventuring Explorers' Club?" said Holly.

Amelia Bedelia just wanted to stop talking and get going, so she made a suggestion. "Let's call it Our Club until we come up with a good name. And let's have a rule. One rule."

what rule???

"What rule?" asked Holly.

"No being bored!" said Amelia Bedelia.

"Yes!" said Holly and Heather together.

"That's settled," said Holly. "Now we need to choose a president."

"I vote for me," said Heather.

"I vote for me too!" said Holly.

They turned to Amelia Bedelia to cast the tie-breaking vote.

"You're leaving me no choice," said Amelia Bedelia. "I have to vote for the smartest, prettiest, most adventuresome explorer I know."

Holly and Heather looked at each other. Then they looked back at Amelia Bedelia. Then they asked, "Who?"

"Me!" said Amelia Bedelia.

5

They all fell over laughing.

"But can we really all be president at the same time?" asked Holly, still giggling.

"We should rotate," said Heather.

"Sure," said Amelia Bedelia. She stood up, turned around in a circle, then sat back down. "My dog does that when she comes into a room and sits."

"I mean," said Heather, "we should take turns."

6

"Okay, you're next," Amelia Bedelia said.

Holly and Heather stood up, turned in a circle, and sat back down. Then they fell against each other, laughing some more.

Heather stopped giggling long enough to ask, "Where should our club meet?"

"We could meet here, in my backyard," said Amelia Bedelia.

"But we're an explorers' club," said Holly. "We have to get out and see new places!"

"Do new things!" agreed Heather.

"Find a cool clubhouse!" said Amelia Bedelia.

"Yeah!" said Holly. "Where we can relax and hang out."

They all went back to thinking.

7

Heather and Holly were thinking about where they could build a clubhouse. Amelia Bedelia was wondering what was so relaxing about hanging out laundry.

"Hey," she said, suddenly. "What is our club all about?"

"Having adventures," said Heather.

"Right," said Amelia Bedelia. "So let's have an adventure. Let's go exploring and discover a clubhouse."

No one had to say another word. They

8

jumped on their bikes, and away they went.

Their adventure took them all over town. But they didn't find any place that seemed just right for a clubhouse. Finally they turned back toward home.

Amelia Bedelia was bringing up the rear as they biked down Pleasant Street, in the oldest neighborhood in town. She slowed down to gaze at the largest house.

It was three stories tall, with skinny windows covered with dark curtains. The paint was peeling, the roof was sagging, and one window on the top floor was cracked. A black cat

sat on the front steps and narrowed yellow eyes at Amelia Bedelia as she rode by.

It looked exactly like a haunted house on a TV show. Amelia Bedelia pedaled faster to get past it and catch up with Holly and Heather.

Her two friends were way ahead, about to turn left. Next to the spooky house was a large vacant lot with an enormous oak tree in the center.

Holly and Heather disappeared around the corner. That was when Amelia Bedelia made an adventurous decision.

Making a sharp left too, she jumped the curb and headed straight into the vacant lot to cut across it diagonally. If she raced through the lot, she could catch up with Holly and Heather.

It was tough to keep her bike rolling over lumpy dirt and knee-high grass. But Amelia Bedelia just pedaled harder. In a few seconds, she would burst out of the bushes ahead of Heather and Holly.

Just as she stood up on her pedals to go as fast as possible, her front tire wedged

11

between a rock and a branch. The front wheel of her bike stopped, but her back wheel kept on going. So did Amelia Bedelia, sailing over her handlebars.

She felt the wind rushing past her ears. Time seemed to slow down, as if she were watching herself in slow motion, soaring free as a bird. Flying upside down certainly was breezy, she thought. But Amelia Bedelia knew that her landing was not going to be easy.

Chapter 2

# Happy Landing

Amelia Bedelia rolled over and opened her eyes. She was lying flat on her back. Out of her right eye, she saw a bright blue sky. Her left eye was looking up into an enormous canopy of green leaves. She had flown for just a few seconds, but here she was looking at the same thing every bird looks at every day—blue sky

to soar through
and branches to rest on.

She checked herself over
to see if anything was broken.

She knew that her two eyes still worked. She lifted her right arm and then her left arm. Okay so far. She lifted her left leg and then her right one. Check. Slowly she sat up and looked around. She was in much better shape than her bike.

Her bike was busted. The front wheel was twisted into something like a figure eight.

"Amelia Bedelia?" shouted Heather.

"Amelia Bedelia!" yelled Holly.

She could hear them, so Amelia Bedelia figured that her ears must be okay too. She answered, "Over here!"

Heather and Holly dropped their bikes on the sidewalk and came running through the empty lot. When they saw Amelia Bedelia next to her crunched bike, they hurried to kneel down beside her.

"Are you okay?" said Holly.

"Why did you ride through this junky lot?" Heather asked.

"I was trying to take a shortcut," answered Amelia Bedelia. She looked at her left knee. It was scraped. She looked at her right elbow. It was bloody. "Only I'm the one who got cut," she added. "From now on, I'm taking only long cuts." Maybe that didn't sound very adventurous, but it would be safer.

"We would have waited for you," said Heather.

"You're lucky you didn't get really hurt," said Holly. "You could have landed on this!" She held up something that looked like a giant rusty corkscrew.

"Or that!" said Heather. She pointed

to a board with nails in it.

There was junk everywhere. Amelia Bedelia hadn't seen it when she had decided to ride through the empty lot, because the long grass and scrubby bushes hid all the trash. But it was there, all right.

"Yikes," said Holly. "Maybe adventure isn't all it's cracked up to be."

"My bike helmet isn't cracked either," said Amelia Bedelia. She took it off and patted it affectionately. "I'm glad I had it on."

Holly helped Amelia Bedelia get to her feet.

Amelia Bedelia hopped a few steps and decided that her sore knee was not too bad. She could walk on it. And that was good, because it looked like she would

**17**

have to walk home.

"Let's go," said Heather. "I don't like this old lot. And that house is spooky."

"You don't like the lot?" asked Amelia Bedelia. "But it's perfect!"

She looked around. So did her friends. They saw:

Tall grass.

Big rocks.

Broken bricks.

Crumbling cinder blocks.

Empty cans.

Bits of metal.

Twists of wire.

Old tires.

Falling-apart chairs.

And a giant oak tree.

Amelia Bedelia limped to the tree. The trunk was so wide her arms could not reach all the way around it. It was so tall that it rose above the houses on either side of the lot. The leaves and branches were so thick that when Amelia Bedelia tipped her head back, she could not see the sky.

"Perfect?" asked Holly. "Perfect for what?"

"For our new clubhouse!" said Amelia Bedelia. "Our explorers' clubhouse!"

Heather looked at Holly. Holly looked at Heather. Heather and Holly both looked at Amelia Bedelia.

"Maybe you'd better sit back down," said Holly. "I think you might have hit your head harder than you thought. Are you *sure* your helmet isn't cracked?"

"I am fine," Amelia Bedelia said. "And so is my helmet. And so is this tree! This is where we should have our clubhouse—a tree house clubhouse."

Holly looked up. So did Heather. Holly started to grin. So did Heather.

"We could get up and down with a ladder," said Holly.

"How about climbing a rope?" said Amelia Bedelia.

"A rope ladder," said Heather.

"Great," said Holly. "We could pull it up after us and be completely on our own. Like we were on a desert island!"

"We could have windows," said Heather.

"A telescope," said Holly. "So we can

see what's happening all over town."

"A hammock!" said Heather. "So we can lie in the sun."

"A roof," said Holly. "So we can rest in the shade."

"A slide for getting down!" said Heather.

"Or a pole for sliding down!" said Holly.

"It's perfect!" said Heather. "Even though you found it by accident, Amelia Bedelia."

"It wasn't that bad an accident," said Amelia Bedelia, rubbing her sore elbow. "And it was totally worth it."

## Chapter 3

# Big Idea, Big Trouble

At dinnertime, Amelia Bedelia let her parents in on her idea. *She* could tell that it was a great idea by how much she was waving her arms around as she told them all about the new club, the vacant lot, and the plans for a tree house. Waving arms always meant that something exciting was about to happen.

But for her parents, Amelia Bedelia's waving arms were a warning, setting off alarm bells, buzzers, and whistles.

"We'll have a rope ladder to get up into the tree house!" Amelia Bedelia said. "We'll have a telescope and windows and a hammock and a balcony! Won't it be great?" She took a big bite of her chicken drumstick and beamed at her mom and dad.

"Well, sweetness," said her mother, "I must say . . ."

But she didn't say anything. She looked over at her husband, and she arched her

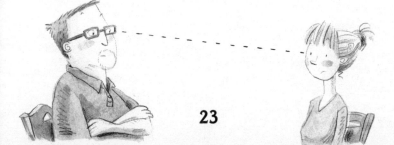

23

right eyebrow in secret parent code. Then she added, "This plan sounds . . . What's the word I'm searching for, honey?"

Amelia Bedelia's father put his fork down. "Unbelievable," he said.

"I knew you'd like it!" said Amelia Bedelia. "It's perfect for us!"

Her father tilted his head so he could look right at her. "Of all the dangerous, hazardous, perilous—"

Amelia Bedelia kept hearing "us" at the end of every word. She interrupted him.

"When I said 'us,' I didn't mean you and me and Mom. Us three girls can handle it."

"Ridiculous!" said her father. "You girls are not

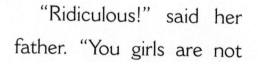

*dangerous! ridiculous! perilous!*
*hazardous! treacherous!*
*perilous!*
*ridiculous!*
*treacherous!*

going to handle anything in that empty lot!" said her father.

"It's not empty," explained Amelia Bedelia. "It's full of trash and stuff."

"Exactly!" said her father.

"Honey," said Amelia Bedelia's mother, "your dad does not think this is a good idea at all, and I don't think you're going to convince him. You're banging your head against a stone wall here."

"I didn't bang my head on anything," said Amelia Bedelia. "Just my elbow and my knee, and I banged them

**25**

on the ground, not a wall."

"You banged your knee?" her
father asked. "You banged your
elbow? How? Where? What happened?"

Amelia Bedelia stood up to show off
the scrapes on her elbow and knee, and
explained how she had done a somersault
over her bike.

"Treacherous!" exclaimed her father.

Amelia Bedelia sat down again. She
was beginning to get the idea that "us"

words were not the friends of explorers. Except, of course, for "adventurous."

"Honey," said her mother, "your dad is right. That lot is no place for children to play. Look what happened to you already. It's not safe."

"I know," agreed Amelia Bedelia. "That's why we have to clean it up!"

Amelia Bedelia could see that her parents still didn't understand. So she followed her number-one rule: she turned to her mother and asked a question.

"Aren't you always telling me we need a sense of community? To give something back to where we are?"

Her mother's eyebrows went up.

"Pleasant Street is just a couple of

blocks away. Isn't that our community?"

Her mother's eyebrows made two tall arches. Her father put his elbows on the table and leaned his forehead on his hands. He sighed.

This, thought Amelia Bedelia, was progress. Time for one more question. "Can't we give back by taking away? Collecting all that junk and recycling and getting rid of the rest?"

Her father sighed again.

"We need to think about this for a minute," Amelia Bedelia's mother said. "Any more questions?"

"Yes," Amelia Bedelia said. "Would you please pass the kale?"

She knew that question would make

28

her mother happy. Every time her mother served them kale, Amelia Bedelia and her father got a lecture about why it was so good for you, along with a helping of the dark green leaves.

Smiling, her mother passed the kale and watched in delight as Amelia Bedelia piled it on her plate. Her father watched carefully. The more kale Amelia Bedelia ate, the less there would be for him.

Amelia Bedelia chewed and chewed.

She tried not to think about what she was eating or how it tasted. Her parents had stopped eating altogether and were staring at each other. They must have been saying things in secret parent code that Amelia Bedelia had not yet worked out, because suddenly her mom spoke.

"All right," said her mother. "You and your friends can clean up that lot. I don't know who owns it, but whoever it is, they haven't done anything with it in years. I'm sure they won't mind if the trash gets taken away. But grown-ups have to be there with you." Then she turned to Amelia Bedelia's father and said, "Honey, I'm sure you wouldn't mind giving up your golf tournament this Saturday to help our

daughter give back to our community, right?"

Amelia Bedelia's father closed his eyes and made a face. He looked as if the idea of giving up his golf game was even more bitter than kale.

"Sweetie, you're asking a whole lot," he said to Amelia Bedelia.

"Of course," Amelia Bedelia agreed. "It wouldn't be any good to clean up just part of the lot. But don't worry. With everyone working together, I'm sure we can clean it up in no time!"

Chapter 4

# One Man's Trash

On Saturday morning, Amelia Bedelia and her parents loaded rakes and shovels, clippers and recycling bins into their car.

First they stopped by a hardware store to get bags for the trash and gloves to protect their hands. "You come back, now!" the clerk called as they walked out the door.

32

"Okay," said Amelia Bedelia. She turned around and headed right back into the store. "Why did you want me to come back?" she asked the clerk. "Did we forget something?"

"Never mind, sweetie," her mother said, coming after her. "Let's get to work!"

They drove to the empty lot. Once they arrived and had unloaded all of their equipment, Amelia Bedelia took a look at her parents in their boots and flannel shirts. Her dad was wearing a hat. Her mom had a bandanna around her neck. Amelia Bedelia looked at herself. She had a flannel shirt and a hat.

"We look like lumberjacks," her father said.

"Could Mom and I be lumberjills?" Amelia Bedelia asked.

Her mom laughed. "We can be anything we want, since we're working hard!" she said. "Here's the plan. Dad and I will move big things to the side of the lot. Tomorrow Heather and Holly and their parents will come by with a pickup truck and haul stuff to the dump. Amelia Bedelia, you're in charge of picking up litter. Let's get to it!"

The first thing Amelia Bedelia's parents found was an old refrigerator.

"Cool!" said Amelia Bedelia.

"Not so cool," said her father as he staggered past her with it. Sweat was dripping down his face.

Amelia Bedelia picked up clumps of newspaper, sneakers without laces, and empty cans and bottles. She stuffed the trash into bags and dumped the paper

in one recycling bin and the bottles and cans in another.

"I'll take that," said her father, reaching out through the broken screen of an old TV and grabbing one of her cans. "I'm glad you brought this in today. How long has it been in your family?"

Amelia Bedelia knew he was pretending to be on his favorite TV show, the one where people brought in junk from the attic and hoped to be told it was worth a million dollars. "About a minute," she told him.

"Well, it's certainly in great condition," her father continued. "It still has the label.

Will you read it for our audience, please?"

"'Grape juice,'" read Amelia Bedelia.

"Right you are," her father said. "This is a spectacular squashed grape juice can. It's priceless! Congratulations!"

"Get the lead out, you two!" called Amelia Bedelia's mother.

"Oh, no, did you find some lead?" Amelia Bedelia asked.

"She means keep working," explained her father. "We're not done."

Her parents cleared away a smelly mattress and a bookcase warped from the rain. Amelia Bedelia found tires. A lot of tires. At least twelve of them. "I'm tired of tires." She sighed.

"Ah," said her father. "That's because you haven't yet been introduced to the fabulous new game of tire bowling."

He set one of the tires on its edge and gave it a big push. It rolled and wobbled toward the end of the lot, bumped into the old refrigerator, and fell over with a *thump*.

"Strike!" he yelled.

Amelia Bedelia hit another tire with her fist.

"No, don't hit. See if you can roll the tire and hit the refrigerator," he said. She did. Pretty soon all the tires were

over on the other end of the lot.

"Wow, look at that pile of junk," he said. "This lot has everything but the kitchen sink!"

"Dad? What's this?" called Amelia Bedelia. She was poking a stick at something behind a scrubby bush.

"Never mind," said her father, coming to look over her shoulder. "That's a kitchen sink."

They carried the kitchen sink over to their junk pile. Amelia Bedelia's mother was already there, leaning against the refrigerator. Amelia Bedelia and her father flopped down for a rest too, and her mom handed them big bottles of

water, which they guzzled down.

"I think that's enough for one day," Amelia Bedelia's mom said.

They loaded the bags of trash and the recycling bins into the car and got ready to go. Amelia Bedelia ran back to give the oak tree a hug and a pat. "We'll be back soon," she whispered to it.

She was facing the spooky old house next to the lot, and she thought she saw movement in one of the windows. A curtain fluttered, as if somebody had lifted it and then dropped it again.

Was somebody at home? And was that person watching them?

## Chapter 5
# Getting a Lot Done

The next day Amelia Bedelia's family drove back to the lot. Heather and Holly were already there with their parents, and a pickup truck was parked at the curb.

"We'll take the refrigerator first," Heather's dad said.

The three girls left the grown-ups talking and wandered away, looking at

their lot. The grass was still high and the weeds were still everywhere, but it didn't look quite as messy as it had before.

"Look! There's a cat!" Holly called out, pointing to a bush.

Amelia Bedelia saw a flash of fluffy gray fur among the leaves.

"We're going to mow the grass around that bush," she said. "I hope the cat doesn't run out and get hurt."

Heather looked worried.

"Maybe we should get it to go away."

"How?" Holly asked.

"Here, kitty!" called Heather.

Amelia Bedelia stuck a hand in the bush, trying to reach the cat's collar. But the cat hissed a warning at her.

Amelia Bedelia grabbed one of the branches. She shook the bush lightly. The cat didn't move. Then Holly shook the bush, and Heather smacked the bush with

a stick, rustling all the leaves. The cat rushed out, darted between Amelia Bedelia's legs, and scampered away.

"Let's get started," Amelia Bedelia's mom called out. "Girls, that goes for you too. No more beating around the bush."

"We're finished," Amelia Bedelia said. "We were just beating the bush to get a cat to run out."

"What?" asked her mother. "Never mind. Grab gloves and let's get to work!"

Heather, Holly, and Amelia Bedelia finished picking up the trash. The three dads made trips to the dump while the three moms mowed the grass and the girls pulled weeds and trimmed bushes.

When the dads returned in the

44

pickup truck, they were very impressed. "This is great," said Holly's father. "I think we can call it a day."

"Why should we call it a day?" asked Amelia Bedelia. "It's a lot."

"I know," he said. "And it looks good."

"It sure does." Holly nodded. "We got a lot done."

"That's what we came here to do," Amelia Bedelia agreed happily.

The lot *did* look great. It would be a wonderful place to build an explorers' clubhouse. The oak tree rose out of a square of smooth grass. There was no trash to be seen anywhere. There were only a few weeds left to be pulled.

"Let's come back next weekend and finish weeding," said Holly. She and Heather and Amelia Bedelia flopped down under the oak tree to rest.

"Girls!" called Holly's mother. "We're making one last trip to the dump. Do you want to ride with us or walk home?"

"Walk!" all three girls called back. They relaxed for a while longer, looking up.

Amelia Bedelia wished she could be in the tree right now, swaying back and forth as the wind rocked the strong, thick branches and rustled the dark green leaves. Being in a tree house would really be easy and breezy, she thought. It would be just like being a bird.

"Pretty soon we'll be able to break ground on our tree house!" said Heather.

"Don't you mean break branch?" asked Holly, and she giggled.

"But if the branches break, our tree house will fall down!" Amelia Bedelia was worried. "We don't want that to happen. Like that lullaby where the cradle falls

47

out of the tree. I always think that's a scary thing to sing to a little baby!"

"Don't worry, Amelia Bedelia," Heather said. "I'm sure no cradles really fall out of trees, and I'm sure our tree house will be very safe too. Let's go get a snack. I'm starving!"

"We can go to Pete's Diner on the way home," Amelia Bedelia said.

The girls got up and walked toward Pete's, thinking of cool milk shakes, hot, crispy french fries, and chocolaty brownies. Amelia Bedelia's stomach rumbled so loudly that a man walking past on the sidewalk turned to look at her.

"Well, bless my bluebottles, if it isn't

48

little Miss Amelia Bedelia!" he exclaimed.
Amelia Bedelia recognized him right away.
It was easy because he was the only person
she knew who wore a ten-gallon hat, like a
cowboy, everywhere he went. His name
was Wild Bill, and he owned a used car lot
on the other side of town.

"How are you, Mr. Bill?" she asked
politely.

"Mighty fine, little lady. You

49

look like you've been hard at work. What have you been up to these days?"

"A lot," said Amelia Bedelia.

Wild Bill looked alarmed. "Not Lots of Lemons again!" he exclaimed.

Amelia Bedelia remembered the lemonade stand she had set up right outside Wild Bill's Auto-Rama. Since she squeezed the juice of one whole lemon into every glass, she made a sign that read LOTS OF LEMONS! Wild Bill had not been happy about that. Amelia Bedelia didn't know that some people used the word "lemon" to mean a used car that didn't work well!

"No, nothing to do with cars," she promised Wild Bill. "My friends and I are

cleaning up a vacant lot.
We're going to build
a clubhouse in a tree."

Wild Bill shook his
head. "If you can pull that
off, just the three of you, I'll eat
my hat!"

"I don't think it would taste
very good," said Amelia Bedelia,
but Wild Bill didn't hear her. He waved
good-bye and went on his way, chuckling
to himself.

The girls reached Pete's and stepped
into the diner. "Amelia Bedelia!" Pete
called out. "Long time no see!"

"That's terrible!" said Amelia Bedelia.
She waved her hand in front of Pete's

face. "What happened to your eyes?"

"My eyes are fine," said Pete. "Just come in and sit down here at the counter and chew the fat! I haven't seen you in a while."

Amelia Bedelia and her friends hopped onto the tall stools at the counter. But Amelia Bedelia hoped that Pete would not actually serve her a plate of fat. Yuck! She'd rather eat french fries any day.

"Milk shakes, please," said Holly.

"I'd like strawberry," said Amelia Bedelia.

"Vanilla!" said Heather.

"Chocolate!" said Holly.

Doris, Amelia Bedelia's favorite waitress, whipped up the milk shakes and brought over three tall glasses. "What have you been up to?" she asked Amelia Bedelia.

"A lot," said Amelia Bedelia.

"I can imagine," said Doris. "You're a good worker. I still remember when you were a waitress in training here. So what's been keeping you so busy?"

"A whole lot," said Amelia Bedelia. "We cleaned up the empty lot on Pleasant Street."

"Good thing you're cleaning up that place. It's an eyesore!" Pete called over from the grill.

"You're right! My eyes got really sore from all the dirt and dust," said Amelia Bedelia, rubbing them.

Pete shook his head and flipped a hamburger, smiling.

"We're going to build a tree house," Holly said.

"And meet in it to talk about what *other* adventures we'd like to have!" Amelia Bedelia added.

"Like skydiving over the Grand Canyon!" said Heather.

"Or scuba diving on the Great Barrier Reef," said Holly.

"What would be your best adventure, Amelia Bedelia?" Heather asked.

Amelia Bedelia thought about it. What would she do? She would take an airplane anywhere she wanted. Flying on an airplane wasn't really as easy and breezy as flying like a bird, but she wouldn't mind. She could pat the nose of the Great Sphinx. She could climb up a zigzaggy pyramid in the jungles of Central America, and swing through the trees with monkeys and macaws. She could ride a scooter through the streets of Rome. Now *that* would feel easy and breezy.

"Come on, Amelia Bedelia," Heather urged. "Tell us!"

"I want to go around the world," Amelia Bedelia said. She sucked up the last of her milk shake, letting her straw make loud slurping noises. "That way I never have to stop exploring!"

Heather and Holly finished up their milk shakes too. "We'd better get going," Holly said, jumping down. "Our parents will be wondering where we are."

The girls paid their bill, said good-bye to Pete and Doris, and headed home.

## Chapter 6

# Suddenly for Sale

Amelia Bedelia slept late the next Saturday, with Finally snuggled up on her bed.

After lunch she hurried to the empty lot. Heather and Holly were there, standing next to a big new sign. It hadn't been there last weekend—Amelia Bedelia was sure of that.

Amelia Bedelia waved from across the street.

"Hi!" she hollered. But Heather and Holly did not wave back. When she reached them, Amelia Bedelia saw why.

A big red sign said FOR SALE in bright white letters.

"For sale?" gasped Amelia Bedelia. "Our lot is for sale?"

 "It isn't ours, really," said Holly miserably. "I guess whoever owns it decided it was time to sell it."

"But now we can't build a tree house here." Heather sighed. After all their hard work! It really didn't seem fair.

"I wish we could buy the lot ourselves," said Holly. "How much do you think it would cost? It's just dirt and grass and stuff."

"And our tree," said Amelia Bedelia,

patting the oak tree gently. "I get three dollars a week for my allowance."

Heather and Holly each got two dollars and fifty cents. "If we put it all together, could we buy the lot?" Holly asked.

The three friends were not sure. But they didn't feel like pulling up weeds anymore. What would be the point?

"Let's go to Pete's," said Amelia Bedelia. "It might make us feel better."

"Back for another round of milk shakes, girls?" asked Doris. Then she saw their sad faces. "Wow," she said. "You look down in the mouth!"

Amelia Bedelia knew this was true. She could feel the corners of her mouth

dragging down in a frown.

Doris whipped up a thick, frothy milk shake with extra chocolate and poured it into a glass. She'd made so much that a little spilled over the lip of the glass and onto the counter. "Whoops!" she said, sticking three straws into the icy drink and setting it down in front of Heather, Holly, and Amelia Bedelia. "This one's on me," she told them, wiping up the spill. "What's wrong?"

"I think the milk shake is really on the

counter," Amelia Bedelia said. "Don't worry; you didn't get any on you. But  what's wrong is that somebody's selling our lot—the one we've been cleaning up for our tree house."

Pete came over and listened as Amelia Bedelia explained about finding the FOR SALE sign. He shook his head. "That's a tough break," he said. "You girls really got the rug pulled out from under you."

"Oh, we didn't have any rugs yet," said Amelia Bedelia. "We hadn't even started on our tree house. But we were almost ready to start."

"Maybe we'll be able

to buy the lot ourselves!" Holly said hopefully. "We thought if we put all our allowances together, we might be able to."

"Hmm," said Pete. "I don't know about that. But if I had any questions about buying and selling some land, there's the person I'd ask."

He pointed to a lady sitting in a booth. She was talking on a cell phone and had a laptop on the table in front of her.

"That's Jill," Pete said. "She's an old friend of mine, and she's a real estate agent—she helps people buy and sell houses and land and things like that."

"Things like our lot?" Amelia Bedelia asked excitedly.

"Just like your lot," said Pete. "You

62

can ask Jill anything you'd like. She's a good person; she'd give you the shirt off her back."

"I don't think it would fit me very well," said Amelia Bedelia. She hopped off the stool and went over to Jill's booth, followed by Holly and Heather, just as Jill finished her call.

Pete introduced her to the three girls. "They've got some questions about real estate," he said, "and I told them you would be able to help."

"Is there such a thing as fake estate?" Amelia Bedelia asked, surprised.

Jill was wearing a bright green shirt. It was a pretty color even if it wouldn't fit a girl, thought Amelia Bedelia. But she still hoped that Jill would not give it to her. That would be embarrassing! Jill also had swinging earrings in her ears and lots of rings on her fingers.

"Well, real estate is just what we call houses or other buildings or land," Jill said cheerfully. "I suppose if somebody tried to sell a house or some land that they didn't really own or that doesn't actually exist, that could be fake estate. But nobody would try a stunt like that with me! I wasn't born yesterday, you know!"

"Oh, yes, I could tell that," said Amelia Bedelia. "I can tell you were born years ago."

"Okay, that's enough!" Jill laughed, which made her earrings swing. "What did you girls want to know?"

They explained about the lot, and Heather asked how much it would cost to buy it. "I can't say for sure," Jill told them. "That's a nice neighborhood. Lots

probably sell at two-fifty, maybe three."

"Great," said Amelia Bedelia. "Holly and Heather both get two-fifty and I get three every week—"

"You do?" said Jill. "You get three hundred thousand dollars every week?"

"Hundred?" asked Holly.

"Thousand?" asked Heather.

"How long would we have to save up our allowances to get just one thousand dollars?" Amelia Bedelia asked her friends.

$2.50 + $2.50 + $3.00 = $8.00 \times 1 \text{ year} =$

"Yikes!" Holly said. "Two-fifty plus two-fifty plus three . . . that's eight dollars a week. If we saved up for a year . . . um . . ."

Jill picked up a calculator. "If you saved

up for a year, you'd have four hundred and twenty-four dollars among you," she said. "I don't think that would be enough to buy your vacant lot."

"Can we do anything else?" asked Holly. "We really wanted that tree house."

"Do you know the name of the realtor who's selling the lot?" Jill asked.

"It was on the sign," Amelia Bedelia said. "I remember. Victor Lee."

"Oh, I know Victor!" Jill said. "I will keep an ear out, girls. And if I hear anything, I'll let you know."

Jill tucked her hair behind her ear as she said that, so Amelia Bedelia knew she'd keep her promise.

## Chapter 7

# Stuck in the Mud

All week in school, Amelia Bedelia thought about adventures. In her mind, she rappelled down Mount Everest and sailed around Cape Horn.

"Where are you, Amelia Bedelia?" her teacher asked. "You're a million miles away."

"My body is right here in the classroom, Mrs. Shauk," said Amelia Bedelia. "But

my brain is going around the world."

"Good thing," said Mrs. Shauk. "Because I'd like your brain to help out with our geography lesson, please. Can you come up to the map and show the class where the Pacific Ocean is?"

That was easy for Amelia Bedelia. But it wasn't so easy to think that their explorers' club would no longer have the perfect easy, breezy place to meet.

The next weekend, she and Holly and

Heather agreed to visit the lot one last time and say good-bye to their oak tree. It rained overnight, but the sun came out in the morning, and Amelia Bedelia set out for the lot, carrying a basket.

When she got there, she saw Holly and Heather sitting sadly by the FOR SALE sign. "What's in the basket, Amelia Bedelia?" asked Holly.

"Lemon tarts!" said Amelia Bedelia. "I baked them this morning."

Amelia Bedelia's lemon tarts were

definitely tart. And also sweet and crunchy and tasty.

"These are really good, Amelia Bedelia," said Holly, munching. "Do you still sell them to Pete for his diner?"

"Sure," said Amelia Bedelia. "I make him a batch every week."

The tarts were delicious, but they were not quite enough to cheer up the girls.

"Amelia Bedelia!" called a loud voice.

Amelia looked up to see her friend Diana strolling by on the sidewalk. Diana was walking five dogs.

"Quick, put the tarts in the basket!" said Amelia Bedelia. She knew how much the dogs that Diana walked for her dog-walking business loved lemon tarts.

There was Sherlock, the bloodhound, with his sad eyes and floppy ears; Dempsey, the boxer, with his blunt nose; Lincoln, the bearded collie, trotting politely by Diana's side; and Snowdrift, the husky, pulling at her leash. There was also a new dog in the pack that Amelia Bedelia had not met before. She was very little, very furry, and black as midnight.

Diana told the dogs to sit, and they sat—except for the new one. That one ran straight to Amelia Bedelia and began sniffing her knees and licking her toes.

"That's Licorice," said Diana. "She's just a puppy, and she isn't doing too well with her training, I'm afraid. She's so friendly that she never wants to sit or stay when there are people to greet!"

"She's sweet!" said Holly, scratching behind Licorice's ears. "Can we play with her? That would cheer us up."

"Sure," said Diana. "But why do you need to be cheered up?"

While Holly and Amelia Bedelia ran around the empty lot with Licorice,

Heather explained to Diana about the tree house they were no longer going to have. Amelia Bedelia, meanwhile, was discovering that playing with a puppy is the perfect way to feel better.

Licorice pounced on sticks and shook them fiercely in her mouth. She chased her tail and yipped with surprise when she caught it. Then she chased Holly. Then she chased Amelia Bedelia. Then she smelled something interesting in a bush. She stopped to sniff— and pulled her leash right out of Amelia Bedelia's hand.

A sleek black cat leaped out
of the bush. The puppy was so surprised
that she tumbled over backward.

The cat dashed for the oak tree.
Licorice dashed after the cat. And Amelia
Bedelia dashed after Licorice.

Amelia Bedelia ran so fast that she
forgot to look where she was going. She
stepped into a patch of mud, slipped, and
flopped down on the seat of her pants.

The cat had scrambled up the oak tree,

but Licorice had already forgotten all about it. She ran back to Amelia Bedelia and bounced into her lap, licking her face and wagging her tail so hard that more mud splattered on Amelia Bedelia. Mud splattered all over Heather and Holly too, when they came running to help Amelia Bedelia up.

"Oh, no!" said Diana. She dropped the leashes for Lincoln, Dempsey, Sherlock, and Snowdrift and hurried over. "I'm so sorry, Amelia Bedelia. Don't tell anybody that the dog I'm supposed to be training got all three of you so dirty. My name will be mud!"

"My pants are mud too!" said Amelia Bedelia.

While Amelia Bedelia was brushing off some of the mud, and while Diana was getting hold of Licorice's leash, a car pulled up next to the lot. Two men got out. One was wearing a baseball cap and jeans. The other was wearing a suit and tie and carrying a clipboard.

"So, Mr. Lee," said the man in the baseball cap, "this is the lot you wanted to show me?"

Chapter 8

# A Perfect Lot

"This is it!" said the man in the suit. "Perfect for any kind of development."

Amelia Bedelia looked at Heather and Holly. Heather and Holly looked at Amelia Bedelia.

"It's him!" whispered Heather. "It's Victor Lee! He's the one who's going to sell our lot!"

"Looks good," said the man in the baseball cap. "Plenty of room to put up a new building. A parking lot too. And a nice neighborhood. I think this would be an excellent place for my dry cleaning business!"

Diana picked up Licorice. Just as she did so, Lincoln, the collie, spotted the black cat that Licorice had chased up the tree. He raced off to run around the oak tree and bark and bark at the cat. The other four grown-up dogs joined him. The cat sat on the branch and stared down at the dogs.

WOOF!

WOOF!

WOOF!

WOOF!

WOOF!

WOOF!

WOOF!

79

"I'm sure it will be perfect," said Victor Lee, raising his voice a little over the barking. "Girls? Excuse me? Do you live in this neighborhood?"

"Yes, we do," said Amelia Bedelia. She and Heather and Holly walked over to where the men were standing.

"Don't you think this neighborhood needs a dry cleaner?" Victor Lee asked hopefully.

"I don't know," said Amelia Bedelia. "I usually wash stuff that I want clean. How can you clean things by drying them?"

But the man in the baseball cap was looking at the three girls and frowning.

"You girls live around here?" he asked. "You sure?"

"Of course we're sure!" said Heather. "We know where we live!"

"Then this lot would not be perfect after all," the man in the baseball cap said firmly. "Why would I open a dry cleaning business in this neighborhood if people go around looking like that?"

He waved a hand at the three muddy girls. Victor Lee looked dismayed.

"No, thank you, Mr. Lee," said the man in the baseball cap. "If you think I'm going to spend money on this lot, you're barking up the wrong tree!"

"I think it's the dogs who are barking," Amelia Bedelia told him. "And it's the right tree. It has the cat in it."

The man shook his head and marched back to the car. Victor Lee looked at the three girls, shook his head too, and drove away. Diana collected her dogs, waved good-bye, and went on with her walk. Amelia Bedelia, Heather, and Holly sat down to finish their lemon tarts.

"That's not the same cat we saw before, is it?" asked Heather.

"No, it's a different one," said Holly. "Do you think it's okay? Can it get down?"

"When it's ready, it will," said Amelia Bedelia. "But maybe we can help it get ready."

She broke off a small piece of lemon tart. She left it at the foot of the tree.

"Lucky cat," said Heather, licking her fingers. "I wish I could have another."

"You can!" said Amelia Bedelia. "I made a bunch!" She handed out more tarts. And they were just beginning to eat them when Victor Lee pulled up again.

He got out of his car and frowned when he saw the girls. "Do you girls play in this lot a lot?" he asked. "Are you planning to go home anytime soon?"

A woman got out of the car and came

to stand by Victor. "Wow, those sure smell good," she said. "What are you girls eating?"

"Lemon tarts," said Amelia Bedelia. "Would you like a taste?" She broke off half of her lemon tart and offered it to the woman.

The woman took a bite. Her eyes went wide, and she shivered a little. "Oh, my!" she said. "That is one tart tart! Did you buy it somewhere around here?"

"No, I made it," said Amelia Bedelia. "But if you want to buy one, I make them for Pete's Diner every week."

"You do?" said the woman. She looked worried for some reason. "Is Pete's Diner near here?"

"Yes," Amelia Bedelia said helpfully. "It's right around the corner. He has wonderful brownies too."

"And milk shakes," added Heather. "The best in town."

"Oh!" the woman said. "That's terrible!"

"How can milk shakes be terrible?" asked Holly.

"Or brownies," added Heather.

"I was planning to open a bakery on this lot," said the woman. "But I don't think anyone would come to it if they can get lemon tarts like these nearby."

"People in this neighborhood really like Pete's Diner," Amelia Bedelia agreed.

The woman looked discouraged. "Mr. Lee, do you have any other lots you could show me?"

She turned back to the car. Victor Lee looked down at the girls. "Do you think you could try not to talk to my clients anymore?" he asked.

Victor Lee and the bakery woman drove away, and the girls finished their tarts. The black cat watched them eat. Then it slowly climbed down the tree and nibbled at the bit of lemon tart that Amelia Bedelia had left on the moss.

"Good kitty!" said Amelia Bedelia. The cat washed its whiskers and trotted through the grass toward the spooky house next door, just as Victor Lee pulled up in his car again! He sighed when he got out and saw that the girls were still sitting by the FOR SALE sign.

This time a man got out of the passenger side of the car. He was wearing a shirt with bright red-and-green parrots on it, and when he spoke, his voice was a little like a parrot's too—harsh and loud.

"This is great!" he said. "This is perfect! This is exactly what I needed!"

Amelia Bedelia exchanged a worried glance with Holly and Heather.

"Excuse me, sir," Amelia Bedelia said. "But we think the lot is perfect too. We like it just the way it is. What are you planning to do to it?"

The man waved his arms.

"I'm going to turn it into a parking lot!" he said. "I'll cut down that big tree, pave it over, and charge people to park here!"

"Cut down the tree!" cried Holly.

"I don't think we need a parking lot in this neighborhood," said Amelia Bedelia. "There's plenty of room already for people to park their cars."

"And lots of people walk," Heather pointed out.

"Or ride bikes," said Holly.

"And fall off them," added Amelia Bedelia.

"Maybe your parents are looking for you girls," said Victor Lee.

"It'll be *perfect*!" shouted the man in the parrot shirt. "I'll charge people to park their cars by the hour, by the day, by the week, by the month. I'll clean up!"

"But we already cleaned up!" Amelia Bedelia exclaimed. "We worked really hard!"

The man in the parrot shirt was not listening. He was grinning, and he got into the car with Victor Lee, still talking about how much money he would make.

Chapter 9

# Minsk and Timbuktu

"What's wrong, sweetie?" Amelia Bedelia's mother asked her that night at dinner. "You look pretty blue."

Amelia Bedelia looked down at her shirt. "I am totally pink," she said. "Except for my red tie-dyed heart."

"Pink looks good," said her mother. "But you look sad. Is something wrong?"

Amelia Bedelia nodded and poked her kale. She told her parents about Mr. Lee finding a buyer for the lot.

"Honey, that's a shame," said her mother. "After all your hard work—our hard work! I can tell you're disappointed."

Her parents exchanged a look in parent code. Her mother tipped her head to one side. Her father's eyebrows moved closer together. It was a look that said, "We're worried about our daughter."

If Amelia Bedelia's parents had been using words, not code, they would have said, "What's happened to Amelia Bedelia? Why isn't she talking a mile a

minute? Why isn't she waving her arms around so fast that kale flies off her fork? Why is she . . . quiet?"

She looked worse than disappointed. She looked discouraged. That was not like Amelia Bedelia at all.

"I just don't see how we can be an explorers' club anymore," Amelia Bedelia said with a sigh. "We needed a cool place to meet. Somewhere different. Somewhere exciting. Somewhere like a tree house. How can we go on adventures if the only place we have to meet is in our own backyards?"

"Your own backyard?" said her father. "I remember when there was a zoo in your very own backyard!"

93

Amelia Bedelia smiled a tiny smile. Her zoo had had a big cat sitting on a fluffy pillow, a frozen gecko in a block of ice, and a genuine monkey. All the neighborhood kids had come. Even her teacher had shown up!

"You of all people don't need a tree house to have adventures," said her mother. "Remember when you rode your bike in the parade? And got chased by all the dogs in town, who wanted to eat up your lemon tarts? And you won a new bike because of it? Now that was an adventure!"

"You'll always be an explorer, Amelia Bedelia," her dad promised her. "You can have adventures right here at home, as long as you're willing to try new things."

"Like kale?" asked Amelia Bedelia, looking down at her plate. She was starting to feel a little better.

"Well . . ." said her father.

Her mom reached over and lifted Amelia Bedelia's plate right off the table.

"You know what?" she said. "I don't think this is a kale day. I think it's a day for tomato salad instead."

After dinner, the phone rang. "Amelia Bedelia!" her mom called. "It's for you!"

"Hi, Amelia Bedelia," said the voice on the other end of the phone. "This is Jill. We met at Pete's Diner the other day. Do you remember?"

"Sure," said Amelia Bedelia.

"Well, I heard something through the

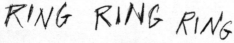

95

grapevine that I thought you might be interested in," said Jill.

Amelia Bedelia wondered how a grapevine could talk. But Jill kept going, so she didn't have a chance to ask.

"The owner of the lot is named Mrs. West, and she lives right next door to it, in a gray three-story house with a big porch out front. You know the one I mean?"

Yes, Amelia Bedelia knew just which one Jill meant. It was the spooky house where she'd had the sense that somebody was watching them from behind the curtains.

"I know Mrs. West—she gives talks at the library sometimes and she's wonderful. Maybe if you spoke to her, she'd wait for a while before selling the lot."

"I don't think so," said Amelia Bedelia with a sigh. She told Jill about Victor Lee and the man who had been so excited about building a parking lot.

"Gee, that's too bad," said Jill. "I'm sorry, Amelia Bedelia. I can tell this means a lot to you."

But Amelia Bedelia couldn't help thinking more about Jill's idea as she got ready for bed. There was a chance, wasn't there, that Mrs. West might change her mind? She should at least try to talk to her. Wasn't that what an adventurer would do?

The next day Amelia Bedelia, Heather, and Holly had a quick club meeting on

Amelia Bedelia's front porch.

"Oh, I don't know, Amelia Bedelia," said Holly. "Will Mrs. West really listen to us? She doesn't even know us, and we're just kids."

"We should try!" insisted Heather. "We're explorers, aren't we?"

"That's right!" said Amelia Bedelia. "And explorers don't give up and turn

back just because their boots start to leak or they run out of food."

"Or the river floods and washes away their jeep," Heather added.

"Or piranhas eat their map," said Amelia Bedelia.

"Or piranhas eat the explorers!" Heather finished.

"Okay! Okay!" said Holly. "I'll come. But I bet Mrs. West won't care about what we think."

"We should probably ask our parents first," said Heather. And that's what they did!

The next day the three friends met at the lot and climbed up the steps of Mrs. West's front porch.

The house still looked a bit spooky to Amelia Bedelia. Not that she believed in ghosts. Or zombies. Or vampires. Or zombie vampire bats with sharp fangs that might swoop down on them from the attic. But still, if she were making a movie about a haunted house, the haunted house would look just like this one.

The porch steps creaked. The doorbell wheezed and sighed instead of ringing.

The door opened slowly.

"Oh, my," said the lady who looked at them through the doorway. She had short white hair, bright purple glasses, and a wide smile. "You're the girls who have been cleaning up my empty lot, aren't you? You did a wonderful job. I wanted to go out

and thank you, but I sprained my ankle in the garden last week, and I haven't been able to walk very well. You haven't seen a cat, have you? Or two?"

"We saw a gray cat in a bush when we were cleaning up," said Heather.

"And we saw a black cat in a tree yesterday," said Holly.

"Those are mine!" said Mrs. West. "The gray one is Timbuktu and the black

one is Minsk. They haven't come in for their food, and that's not like them. I'm a bit worried. But I've forgotten my manners! Come in, girls, come in."

Leaning on a cane, Mrs. West ushered the girls into a wide front hallway. "Wow!" said Amelia Bedelia, looking around.

"Zowie!" added Heather.

"Yikes!" said Holly.

There was a beautiful rug with tassels on the floor. A mirror, whose frame had been carved with hundreds of tiny flowers, hung on one wall. Amelia Bedelia could see pictures of the pyramids of Egypt and the Eiffel Tower and a huge red rock sticking up out of flat desert land. She saw photos

of tall churches built of stone, and a city that seemed to have rivers instead of streets, and a marketplace where stalls were heaped with golden marigolds and women wore saris as bright as the flowers. She saw monkeys swinging through tall green trees, and giraffes ambling across grassy plains, and penguins sliding across slippery ice.

"Now, what can I do for you girls?" asked Mrs. West. "Besides saying thank you for such a lot of work."

"Maybe we can do something for you first," said Amelia Bedelia. "Can we help find your cats?"

"That would be wonderful!" said Mrs. West. "I'm worried they might

**103**

have gotten up into the attic. My ankle is still bothering me, and the attic stairs are quite steep. I don't think I could climb them. Would you mind checking?"

"We don't mind," said Amelia Bedelia.

Mrs. West showed them the way up to the second floor. There was a huge wooden horn hanging on the wall above the staircase. Amelia Bedelia ran her fingers along it as they climbed.

"Here's the door to the attic," Mrs. West said.

The door was a little bit open. Amelia Bedelia pushed it open all the way and looked up a narrow, dusty flight of stairs.

She could see two trails of little paw prints in the dust. It looked like the cats really had gone this way.

But the stairs looked rickety . . . and kind of spooky.

Amelia Bedelia wanted to help Mrs. West. Her mother had remembered that Mrs. West used to take classes at the yoga studio and that she was funny and interesting. Amelia Bedelia wanted to find Timbuktu and Minsk. She didn't want to be a scaredy-cat. For a moment she imagined herself with whiskers and pointy ears, cowering under a bed.

No, that wasn't how an explorer acted. If two real cats could go up into that creepy attic, couldn't an adventurer like Amelia Bedelia follow them?

Chapter 10

# A New Explorer

"You go first, Amelia Bedelia," Holly said, peering up the attic stairs over Amelia Bedelia's shoulder.

"Why me?" asked Amelia Bedelia.

"You're president today," said Holly.

"I am?" asked Amelia Bedelia.

"Sure," Heather said nervously.

Amelia Bedelia sighed. If she was

president of an explorers' club, she really
had no choice.

"Here, Timbuktu! Here, Minsk!" she
called as she climbed up the creaky stairs.

At the top, she stepped out into a
wide, dusty space. And she screamed.

Actually, it came out as a squeak. A
huge face with dark, scary eyes
and a long, skinny nose was

laughing at her from the far wall.

Holly yelped—before all three girls realized that what they were looking at was a wooden mask.

"Oh, gosh," said Holly. "My heart's in my mouth!"

Amelia Bedelia's heart was where it usually was . . . but it was thumping.

There were lots of old trunks in the attic, and piles of boxes. Cobwebs swung from the rafters overhead.

Amelia Bedelia followed the paw prints, trying not to think of ghosts or goblins or vampire bats. Or vampire cats!

Something brushed the top of Amelia Bedelia's hair, like a ghostly hand. She squeaked again, and Heather grabbed her shoulder.

Amelia Bedelia looked up. A kite with a long, dangling tail hung from the ceiling. A fierce face with a scowling mouth was painted on it.

"Yikes!" whispered Holly.

But Amelia Bedelia was starting to feel braver. A kite and a mask and cobwebs and shadows were not enough to stop true explorers! She tiptoed past a bucket. She saw more pails and buckets in other spots around the attic. She looked up. There were holes in the roof.

The paw print trail led across the attic to a half-open window. There were more paw prints on the sill.

"I bet the cats went out the window!" Holly said.

"I'm sure they did," said Amelia Bedelia.

"How can you be so sure?" asked Heather.

Amelia Bedelia pointed. "Because I see them over there," she said.

The three girls crowded around the window and looked out.

Next to Mrs. West's house was a smaller building. As they watched, the girls saw a fluffy gray shape leap across the gap between the house and the smaller building and land on the roof. A sleek black shape was already there, waiting.

The two cats walked across the roof of the other building and disappeared.

"The cat's out of the bag!" said Holly, and giggled.

"I think both cats are out of the attic," said Amelia Bedelia.

"I meant, now we know the secret of where the cats are," said Holly. "Let's tell Mrs. West!"

"The carriage house!" exclaimed Mrs. West when the girls told her what they had seen. "Oh, thank you, girls! I never would have thought to check there. Follow me!"

The girls followed Mrs. West outside and into the other building. Amelia Bedelia

meow meow
meow
meow
meow me

looked around, but to her surprise, she didn't see any carriages. Just two very old-looking cars.

Soft meows came from a loft overhead. "That's where those cats are!" said Mrs. West, shaking her head. "How will we ever get them to come down?"

There was a ladder leading up to the loft. "We could climb up," said Holly.

"But could we climb down while we're holding cats?" asked Heather.

"I have a better idea!" Amelia Bedelia

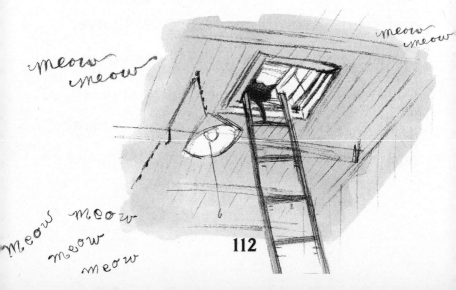

meow meow

meow meow

meow meow
meow
meow

said. "Do you have any  lemons?" she asked Mrs. West.

Mrs. West did have lemons. Better than that, she had lemon marmalade and sugar cookies. Amelia Bedelia spread a little marmalade on a cookie and left it at the foot of the ladder. Then the three girls and Mrs. West waited.

"Wow," said Heather. "Look at these cars. They look old!"

"Just like me," Mrs. West agreed.

One of the cars was a convertible, silver and sleek and curvy. It looked almost as if it would float or fly as well as it could drive. The other car was square and boxy, with big spoked wheels and a steering wheel on a stick.

"My husband loved old cars," said Mrs. West. "These were the last two in his collection. Nobody else in my family has room to keep them. I've been trying to sell them, but it takes such a long time to find the right buyer for cars like these. They're white elephants, really."

Amelia Bedelia looked hard at the cars, but she could not see any long dangling trunks or big floppy ears.

Just then there was a quiet meow from the top of the ladder, and a black, whiskered face poked out of the loft.

"That's Minsk!" whispered Mrs. West.

Slowly, rung by rung, Minsk eased himself down the ladder until he could start licking the marmalade off the cookie.

The gray, fluffy cat appeared and meowed. "Timbuktu!" Mrs. West said.

Timbuktu scampered down the ladder and pushed Minsk aside so that she could also have a bite of lemon marmalade.

"Thank goodness!" said Mrs. West. She scooped up Minsk. Amelia Bedelia picked up Timbuktu. "Bring her inside, would you?" asked

Mrs. West. "Then I can pour you some lemonade to thank you for your help!"

They carried the cats back into the house. Amelia Bedelia paused in the front hallway to look again at the pictures on the wall. One in particular caught her eye. In it, a woman was standing on the edge of an enormous canyon, waving. She had glasses and short hair and she looked a lot like . . .

"That's you!" said Amelia Bedelia.

"Yes, it is!" Mrs. West smiled even more widely. "Good eye. My husband took those pictures. He was a wonderful photographer."

"Have you really been to all these places?" Amelia Bedelia asked.

116

"Certainly," said Mrs. West. "When I was a bit younger, of course. My husband and I loved to travel together."

"Wow," said Amelia Bedelia again. "You must have been around the world!"

Mrs. West laughed. "More than once!" she said. "But come into the kitchen, girls. I'll feed these silly cats and pour you some lemonade, and you can tell me what you wanted to see me about."

## Chapter 11

# Another Woman's Treasure

Mrs. West poured tall glasses of icy lemonade and set out sugar cookies. "First, tell me how you knew my cats would like lemon marmalade," she said.

"Because we knew that Minsk, at least, likes lemon tarts!" said Amelia Bedelia. She explained how she had coaxed Minsk down out of a tree with one of her tarts.

Then the girls told Mrs. West about their club, and how a tree house would be a perfect meeting place, and how the oak tree in her lot would be the perfect place for that tree house.

"So we were wondering . . . maybe . . ." Amelia Bedelia said. "Could you *not* sell the lot after all?"

"Oh, dear." Mrs. West sighed. "I'm sorry, girls, but the truth is, I need the money. I want to stay in this house as long as I can. It's full of wonderful memories and all the things my husband and I collected in our travels. But the roof has started to leak, and I need to repair it quickly. There are some other things around the house that need work also.

That's why I decided to sell the lot."

Amelia Bedelia felt terrible.

"It's a shame." Mrs. West finished up her glass of lemonade. "I wish I could help out three fellow explorers. Would you like to see some things we collected on our travels? I imagine you saw my mask from Nigeria up in the attic, and the kite from Japan too. There are some other interesting mementoes I could show you."

"I'd love to see them," said Heather.

"Yes, please!" said Holly.

Amelia Bedelia was not sure. "Did you really bring home toes?" she asked. "And just men's toes, or are there any from women?"

Mrs. West laughed. "'Mementoes'

**120**

is another word for souvenirs. Things that I've collected from all over."

"In that case," said Amelia Bedelia, "I'd love to see them too."

Mrs. West told them that the wooden horn hanging above the staircase was a didgeridoo from Australia. There were swords from Spain hanging in the library, and a fan made of peacock feathers on a desk. Next to the fan was a jar full of coins from countries all over the world,

and also a giant shell, shiny pink inside, that Mrs. West had found in Bermuda. When Amelia Bedelia held it up to her ear, she could hear the sea.

"I'm sorry that I couldn't help with your tree house," Mrs. West told them when it was time for them to leave. "Do come back another day. I love having company."

The three friends headed home. Amelia Bedelia took a last look at Mrs. West's house as they walked down the block. It did not look spooky to her anymore. It looked like a house full of treasures, like a wonderful place to explore.

"That was exciting!" said Holly. "I loved that long horn thing the best. What did Mrs. West call it?"

"A didgeridoo," said Heather.

"Is there a didgeridon't?" asked Amelia Bedelia.

"I liked the kite in the attic," said Holly.

"I liked all of it," said Amelia Bedelia. "I understand why Mrs. West wants to stay in her house, with all those cool souvenirs and mementoes. But I wish there was some way we could have the tree house

*and* Mrs. West could have the money she needs to fix up her home at the same time!"

That night Amelia Bedelia perched on a stool in the kitchen, tearing up lettuce for a salad and telling her parents all about her visit to Mrs. West's house. She described the photographs, the kite, the swords, the didgeridoo, and finally the cars in the garage.

"They're really neat," she said, dumping the lettuce into a bowl. "But Mrs. West says nobody in her family wants them."

"Can you toss the salad, Amelia Bedelia?" asked her father.

Amelia Bedelia picked up the bowl of salad and eyed the ceiling. "How high?" she asked.

"I mean, put some dressing on it and use the tongs to gently shake things around so the dressing gets on every vegetable," said her father. "And about the cars, just remember—one man's trash is another man's treasure."

"The cars are not treasure," said Amelia Bedelia. "And they are not carriages or elephants either. They're just cars, but pretty cool old ones. Plus, they belong to Mrs. West, and she is a woman, not a man."

"Some cars can be treasure," her father explained. "Valuable. Worth a lot of money."

"How much money?" asked Amelia Bedelia.

"No idea," said her father. "I don't know that much about old cars."

"But I bet your friend Wild Bill does," said her mother. "Why don't you ask him?"

The next morning Amelia Bedelia woke up to the sound of leaves brushing against her window. The wind had picked up, and the trees were dancing.

Something inside Amelia Bedelia was dancing too—excitement! She dialed Wild Bill's number, thinking about those cool old cars in Mrs. West's carriage house. Her dad had said cars could be treasures, hadn't he? And Mrs. West needed money, didn't she? What if those old cars really were valuable? Maybe Mrs. West would

not have to sell the lot! Maybe there was a tree house in Amelia Bedelia's future, after all!

"Howdy!" said a voice on the phone. "Thank you for calling Wild Bill's Auto-Rama, the home of the sweet deal! Are you in the market for a new car today?"

"Actually, no," said Amelia Bedelia. "I'm at home."

"I know who this is," said Wild Bill. "Amelia Bedelia, right?"

"That's right," said Amelia Bedelia. "And I have a question for you. I know someone who has two cars. Old ones. I was wondering if they might be worth a lot of money."

"Lots of people have old cars in their

garages, little lady," said Wild Bill. "And usually they're not worth one red cent."

"I don't think these would be worth one cent, no matter what color it is," Amelia Bedelia agreed. "I think they might be worth lots of dollars. One of them looks really old. It has a steering wheel on a stick. And the other one is silver and curvy and shiny. On the front it says something that starts with an F. Furry . . . no, Ferrari."

"What? What? What?" shouted Wild Bill into the phone.

"Ferrari!" Amelia Bedelia shouted back.

"Little lady, meet me right away at your friend's house! Tell me where it is!" Wild Bill exclaimed. "And hold on to your hat! This could be very exciting!"

Amelia Bedelia told her parents where she was going and hurried over to Mrs. West's. The wind whistled past her ears and tugged at her baseball cap.

When she got there, Wild Bill was waiting by the carriage house with Mrs. West. Amelia Bedelia waved to them and clamped her hands together on the top of her head.

"What are you doing?" Wild Bill asked.

"I'm hanging on to my hat, like you said," Amelia Bedelia explained. "Or else the wind might blow it away." She looked up at him. "Or I guess you might eat it."

"Ma'am, can we see those cars?" Wild Bill asked

Mrs. West. "I was happy to wait for this little lady, but I tell you, I'm so excited I've got ants in my pants!"

Amelia Bedelia took a step back. "How did they get in there?" she asked.

Smiling, Mrs. West unlocked the carriage house door.

"Jumping Jehoshaphat!" Wild Bill exclaimed. "I don't believe it!"

He ran into the carriage house. He circled around the cars. He peered underneath them. He peeked under the hoods. He was beaming.

"Ma'am," he said to Mrs. West, "I'd be very honored to sell these cars for you."

"Well!" Mrs. West was smiling too. "I can hardly believe it! Perhaps they'll bring in enough to let me make the repairs my house needs. What a windfall!"

"Did you fall?" asked Amelia Bedelia, concerned. "Did the wind push you over?"

"No," said Mrs. West, laughing. "This is just the best news I've had in a long time—all thanks to you, Amelia Bedelia!"

That night, before dinner, the phone rang. It was Mrs. West. "Guess what,

Amelia Bedelia?" she said. "Your friend Wild Bill found a buyer for my cars right away. With the money from the sale, I'll be able to make my repairs."

"That's great," said Amelia Bedelia.

"So I don't have to sell my lot," Mrs. West went on. "In fact, I've decided to donate that land to the community to be made into a park."

"That's really great!" said Amelia Bedelia. "A park to play in is way better than a place to park cars!"

## Chapter 12

# Here's to Amelia Bedelia!

One bright and sunny morning not too long after Mrs. West sold her cars, Amelia Bedelia jumped out of bed and did a little dance with Finally. The big day was here at last. She could hardly wait!

First, Heather and Holly and

their parents drove to Amelia Bedelia's house. The girls were so excited that they skipped and ran and turned cartwheels in the yard while the grown-ups talked.

But finally everybody was ready. The girls jumped on their bikes. The moms and dads walked behind. Amelia Bedelia's mom carried a large white box, and her dad held Finally's leash.

Amelia Bedelia felt easy and breezy, zipping along. She led the way right to the empty lot next to Mrs. West's house. Only it wasn't an empty lot anymore.

Today was the new park's opening day!

Amelia Bedelia braked her bike and coasted to a stop. Heather and Holly were right behind her.

"Wow," Holly whispered.

"Amazing!" Heather added. "I didn't think it would be this good!"

"I did," said Amelia Bedelia, looking around with a satisfied smile. "I knew it would be the best park in town!"

It was a park made for adventures. There were curving, swooping lanes for riding bikes. There was a wall to practice rock climbing. There were nets and ladders made of rope to clamber up and long, long ropes to swing on. There was a fountain kids could splash in. And best of all, there was—

"Our tree house!" Holly exclaimed.

It was the best tree house in the world. Amelia Bedelia was sure of it. It had everything the girls had talked about: a rope ladder, a hammock, a telescope,

and two ways to get down—a slide and a pole. It was the perfect place for an explorers' club to meet.

A little black dog with long legs came dashing up to sniff Finally. Diana came running after her. "Sorry!" she gasped. "Licorice is very excited about this new park!"

"We are too!" said Amelia Bedelia.

Everyone in the neighborhood was excited. The park was full of parents and kids. Pete was trying out the climbing wall. Doris was cheering him on. Amelia Bedelia waved at her friend Charlie, who was chasing his poodle, Pierre, through the fountain. Mrs. West was sitting on a

bench, looking around with a wide smile, and Wild Bill was at her side.

"Here you go, Amelia Bedelia," said her mother, handing her the large white box.

Amelia Bedelia took the box and brought it over to Wild Bill.

"Howdy!" said Wild Bill. Mrs. West gave Amelia Bedelia a kiss on the cheek.

"Howdy!" Amelia Bedelia said back. "I brought something for you!" And she handed the box to Wild Bill.

"For me?" Wild Bill looked surprised.

He opened the box carefully. First he smiled. Then he started to laugh out loud.

"Look what this little lady has done in her kitchen!" he chortled.

Inside the box was a cake in the shape of a hat—a ten-gallon cowboy hat.

"You said you'd eat your hat if we cleaned up this lot and got a tree house here," said Amelia Bedelia. "And we did!"

Amelia Bedelia's parents had forks and paper plates too. Wild Bill served pieces of his cake hat, chuckling all the while.

"A toast!" he said, holding up a piece of cake on a fork.

"No, it's cake," said Amelia Bedelia.

"Chocolate with marshmallow frosting."

Wild Bill shook his head. "A toast means that we honor somebody who has done something extraordinary," he said. "And this toast is for you. To Miss Amelia Bedelia and her friends! They did a lot to make this new park happen!"

"To Amelia Bedelia and her friends!" everyone in the park called out, and Amelia Bedelia blushed.

Amelia Bedelia and Heather and Holly sat down on the bench beside Mrs. West to eat cake and watch people enjoying the park. "We want to ask you something," said Heather to Mrs. West.

"And tell you something," Amelia Bedelia added.

"Go right ahead!" Mrs. West said cheerfully.

"We found a name for our club at last," said Amelia Bedelia. "We are going to be the Easy Breezy East and West Explorers' Club!"

"Perfect," said Mrs. West, smiling. "And what did you want to ask?"

"Will you be in the club too?" Holly asked. "You're the best explorer we know."

"I'd be honored," Mrs. West answered.

"We'll meet in the tree house in the summer," said Holly.

"And in the winter we can meet in my house!" said Mrs. West.

"Will you tell us some more about your adventures?" asked Heather.

"I certainly will," said Mrs. West. "And we will all follow the first and only rule of the Easy Breezy East and West Explorers' Club . . ."

"No being bored!" all four explorers shouted together.

"Explorers rule!" added Amelia Bedelia.

# Two Ways to Say It

## By Amelia Bedelia

"No more beating around the bush."

"Stop wasting time."

"It's an eyesore."

"It's really ugly."

"The cat's out of the bag!"

"Everyone knows the secret!

"I'll eat my hat!"

"I'll be super surprised!"

"My name will be mud!"

"I'll be in big trouble!"

"You're barking up the wrong tree."

"You are totally wrong."

"You're a million miles away."

"You aren't paying attention."

"Hold on to your hat!"

"It's going to get exciting!"

"You girls really got the rug pulled out from under you."

"Someone upset your plans."

"I'm so excited I've got ants in my pants!"

"I'm so excited I can't stand still!"

145

#5

# Amelia Bedelia
## Shapes Up

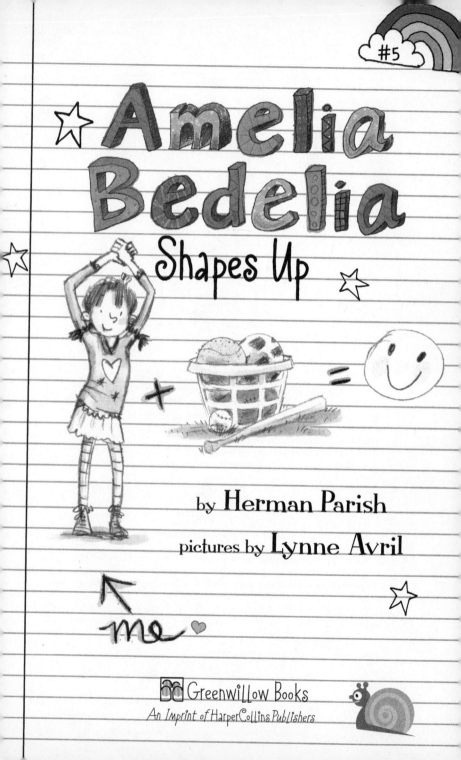

by Herman Parish

pictures by Lynne Avril

← me ♡

Greenwillow Books
An Imprint of HarperCollins Publishers

Gouache and black pencil were used to prepare the black-and-white art.

Amelia Bedelia is a registered trademark of Peppermint Partners, LLC.

The Library of Congress has cataloged an earlier printing of this title as follows:

Parish, Herman.

Amelia Bedelia shapes up / by Herman Parish ; pictures by Lynne Avril.

pages cm.—(Amelia Bedelia ; #5)

Summary: Picked last for kickball, Amelia Bedelia gets another chance to prove her athleticism when her class holds a mini-Oylympics.

ISBN 978-0-06-233397-1 (hardback)—ISBN 978-0-06-233396-4 (pbk. ed.)—ISBN 978-0-06-233399-5 (pob)

[1. Sports—Fiction. 2. Schools—Fiction. 3. Humorous stories.] I. Avril, Lynne, (date) illustrator. II. Title.

PZ7.P2185Arbe 2014 [Fic]—dc23 2014008703

15 16 17 18 19 CG/RRDH 10 9 8 7 6 5 4 3 2 1

ISBN 978-0-06-240368-1 (Amelia Bedelia Bindup #5 and #6)

Greenwillow Books, *An Imprint of* HarperCollins*Publishers*

Ages 6–10. Cover art © 2014, 2015 by Lynne Avril. Cover design by Sylvie Le Floc'h.

Also available as an ebook. www.ameliabedeliabooks.com

For Skip Flanagan—

*always* in shape—H. P.

For Jim and Marybeth—L. A.

# Contents

## Chapter 1

# Heads Up!

Amelia Bedelia did not wake up and say to herself, *Gee, what a beautiful day. I can't wait to look silly in front of all my friends.*

Amelia Bedelia would never wish that on anyone, much less herself. But that is exactly what happened. Doubly worse, it happened twice!

$$\frac{3}{4} = \frac{6}{8}$$

$$\frac{2}{8} = \frac{1}{4}$$

After doing fractions all morning, Amelia Bedelia and her friends were ready for recess. When Mrs. Robbins let them out early, they raced to the playground.

"Last one to the water fountain has to add up ten fractions, except Amelia Bedelia!" yelled Rose.

Rose was making an exception for Amelia Bedelia because Amelia Bedelia was the reason they had gotten out early for recess. She had given their math teacher,

$\neq$

$1 = 8$

Mrs. Robbins, a headache. Here's why:

"Amelia Bedelia," said Mrs. Robbins at the beginning of math class, "what if I gave you a pie—"

"Thank you," said Amelia Bedelia. "I love pie."

"I'm not really giving you a pie," said Mrs. Robbins. "Just pretend."

"Okay," said Amelia Bedelia.

Mrs. Robbins continued, "Now suppose eight people want a piece."

"No problem," said Amelia Bedelia. "I'd cut it into eight equal pieces."

"That's correct," said Mrs. Robbins. "But what if you had served half the pie,

3

and then four more people showed up?"

"I'd bake them cupcakes," said Amelia Bedelia. "Pretend cupcakes."

"Pretend you can't bake," said Mrs. Robbins. "Stick with the pie. What fraction would the others get?"

"I've never tasted fraction pie," said Amelia Bedelia. "Is it good?

"A fraction isn't a flavor," said Mrs. Robbins. "It is a piece of the whole."

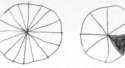

"But holes are empty," said Amelia Bedelia. "Am I serving pieces of nothing?"

"I mean the whole pie," said Mrs. Robbins. "I'll give you a hint. Half of the pie is gone, right? So you'd cut the other half into eight pieces—eight sixteenths, which is equal to four eighths, or two quarters."

"Then that's easy," said Amelia Bedelia. "If half a pie is just two quarters, I'd spend fifty cents and buy another half a pie for the new people."

"Pretend you don't have any cents," said Mrs. Robbins.

"I don't have to pretend that," said

$\frac{8}{16} = \frac{4}{8} = \frac{2}{4} = \frac{1}{2}$   5

$\frac{8}{16} = \frac{1}{2}$

$$\frac{8}{16} = \frac{4}{8} = \frac{2}{4} = \frac{1}{2}$$

$$\frac{8}{16} = \frac{1}{2}$$

Amelia Bedelia. "Sharing one puny pie with twelve people makes no sense at all."

The other kids had been trying not to laugh all along, but now they laughed out

loud. Mrs. Robbins was not laughing. She was rubbing her forehead.

"Pretend you know everything there is to know about fractions," Mrs. Robbins said with a sigh. "We'll try this again tomorrow. I think we all deserve an early recess."

This was too good to be true. No one moved a muscle until Mrs. Robbins added, "I'm not pretending!"

Amelia Bedelia and her friends took turns drinking from the water fountain. Then Rose and Dawn picked teams for a game of kickball. One after another, girls joined Rose or Dawn on the field until only Amelia Bedelia was left.

It was Dawn's turn, and Amelia Bedelia began jogging toward her.

"I choose the water fountain," said Dawn.

Amelia Bedelia stopped in her tracks. The other girls burst out laughing.

"That's mean," said Rose. "You have to pick Amelia Bedelia."

"Why?" asked Dawn. "She makes mistakes. Last time, we lost because of her. At least a water fountain won't goof up."

"I'll tell you why," said Rose. "If the water fountain is on your team, then my team can't get a drink without your permission. The water

8

fountain is for everybody. That's why Amelia Bedelia is for you."

Amelia Bedelia's cheeks were getting redder and redder. She had never felt so embarrassed in her entire life. How could she come in second place to a rusty, leaky water fountain? Weren't they all friends? Had Dawn forgotten that she had feelings?

Dawn just shook her head. Then she motioned for Amelia Bedelia to come over and join her. Amelia Bedelia felt like running the other way, running all the way home. Instead she nodded, put a smile on her face,

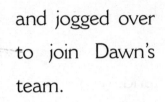

and jogged over to join Dawn's team.

Dawn put Amelia Bedelia in the outfield—the way, *way* out outfield. Amelia Bedelia stood there by herself for the entire game. But right before recess ended, Holly kicked the ball with all her might. It soared up, up, up in a high arc until it was a tiny dot, like a period at the end of a sentence. Then it began falling down, down, down toward Amelia Bedelia.

"Catch it!" hollered Dawn from the pitcher's mound. "Catch it and we win!"

Amelia Bedelia put her arms up and ran toward where she thought the ball would land. The sun was right in her eyes. She had to remind herself that it was just a red bouncy ball she was hoping to catch, and not a fiery asteroid screaming toward earth. She could do it. She could catch it! But it hurt to look into the sun and try to see the ball. Her eyes were watering. Amelia Bedelia blinked, glancing at the ground for just a second. She glimpsed Holly rounding second base on her way home with the winning run. . . .

*BO-INNNNG!* The ball hit the top of Amelia Bedelia's head so hard it knocked her on her butt. The ball bounced back up in the air. Penny made a diving catch,

right before the ball hit the ground. Holly was out. Game over. They'd won!

Everyone ran to Amelia Bedelia to make sure she was all right. Dawn helped her up while Penny brushed the dirt and grass off her back.

"Awesome teamwork!" said Dawn. "Amelia Bedelia, you can be on my side any day."

Yay!

Chapter 2

Water ~~Boy~~ Girl

When Amelia Bedelia got home from school, Dawn's remark about the water fountain was still bothering her. How dare Dawn pick a crummy water fountain for her team before picking her? Dawn was her friend! It

13

*6 x 2 knees = double <u>ouch</u>!*

reminded Amelia Bedelia of the time she had skinned both her knees at the beach and then went swimming. The salt water had really stung! Only now her feelings were hurting, not her knees.

After Amelia Bedelia set the table for dinner, she went outside and sat on the front steps. Her dog, Finally, sat down next to her and put her paw on her knee. Amelia Bedelia scratched Finally's furry ears. They waited for her father to come home from work. He always had some joke or said something wacky. Her

dad could always cheer her up.

She did not have to wait long. As he was turning off the sidewalk and onto their front walk, he bellowed loud enough for the neighbors to hear, "Hello, Amelia Bedelia! How's my favorite daughter?"

"I'm your only daughter," she said.

"Shhhh!" said her father as they sat down together on the steps. He leaned close, and in a fake whisper he said, "Don't

tell your twelve sisters. They get so jealous."

The thought of having twelve sisters was so preposterous that it made Amelia Bedelia smile.

"So, how was school?" asked her father.

"School was fine," said Amelia Bedelia. "Recess was terrible."

"Be glad you still have recess," he said. "I wish I did. I'm glad it's Friday."

"How's work?" asked Amelia Bedelia.

"Another day, another dollar," he said.

"You need a raise, Dad," said Amelia Bedelia.

"I'm just bringing home the bacon," he

said. "Keeping the wolf from our door."

"Save the bacon for tomorrow," said Amelia Bedelia. "We're having chicken tonight."

Her father's stomach growled loudly.

"Yipes," said Amelia Bedelia. "Sounds like you brought home a wolf with the bacon."

"Wolves love bacon," he said, patting his stomach. "I'll huff, and I'll puff, and—"

"I'll blow your house down!" shouted Amelia Bedelia.

# BANG!

BANG went their front door as it swung open and hit the side of the house. Amelia Bedelia and her father jumped up.

"Hey, you two!" said Amelia Bedelia's mother from the doorway. "I'm struggling to fix dinner, and here are my best helpers, sitting around having recess."

"I wish," said Amelia Bedelia's father.

"I don't," said Amelia Bedelia.

"Dad, could you carve the chicken for us?" asked Amelia Bedelia's mother. "And Amelia Bedelia, please fill the glasses with water."

"Maybe you should install a water fountain," said Amelia Bedelia.

"Don't be silly," said her

mother. "Who needs a water fountain when I've got you?"

Amelia Bedelia's heart sank, but she did what she was told.

During dinner, Amelia Bedelia told her parents what had happened at recess. She tried to laugh about it, but her parents weren't laughing. They were glancing at each other, the way parents do when they want to talk without kids around.

Amelia Bedelia finished her story by saying, "So I don't feel like filling up water glasses right now, like a water fountain."

"I'm so sorry, sweetie," said her mother. "I didn't mean to hurt your feelings."

"I know," said Amelia Bedelia as she got up from the table. "I'm going to bed. This day has been way too long." She cleared her place and headed to her room.

## Chapter 3

# Little Pitchers Have Red Ears

Amelia Bedelia tried her best to go to sleep, but it was way too early for that. Plus, she kept hearing her mother and father saying her name, again and again.

Was something wrong?

Was she in trouble?

21

Why were they talking about her?

Amelia Bedelia slipped out of bed and tiptoed down the hall to the top of the stairs. She poked her face between the spindles on the stairway. Now she could

hear everything her parents were saying.

"Amelia Bedelia seems fine to me," said her mother. "But maybe she's having coordination problems."

*What kind of problems?* Amelia Bedelia looked down at her pajamas. The bottoms matched the top perfectly. All her outfits were coordinated. She loved matching colors and patterns and—

"She could get stronger," said her father. "You know, get in shape."

Amelia Bedelia looked at herself again. This *was* her shape, the only shape

she had. She wasn't a jellyfish or an octopus or a cat. She was a girl.

"Maybe she's just not that interested in sports," said her mother.

Amelia Bedelia almost shouted "Bingo!" She liked sports, but she wasn't crazy about them. Why should she be? In her last try at sports, she had come in second to a crummy water fountain. And now her own parents thought she should get coordinated into a new shape.

"One thing is certain," said her mother. "The corners of her mouth are droopy. That means that our cupcake is unhappy."

"Unhappy!" exclaimed her father.

"*Shhh!*" said her mother. "She'll hear

*Shhh!!*

you. Little pitchers have big ears."

Amelia Bedelia was puzzled. Had she heard that right? Did her mom want Amelia Bedelia to be a pitcher and play baseball? Or was she saying that Amelia Bedelia had big ears?

"She has lots of friends," said her father in a quieter voice. "All the kids love her."

"True," said her mother. "But if you were always the last one picked for a team, you might not love yourself."

Her parents were talking softly now, so Amelia Bedelia had to strain to hear them. She pressed her face between the spindles as far as she could and tilted her ear toward the kitchen. She

Pop! Pop-pop Pop-pop Pop!

caught words like "self-confidence" and "sports camp."

Then she heard a pop. *Pop . . . pop-pop!*
*POP-POP-POP!* Her mom was making popcorn for just the two of them.

The wonderful aroma of freshly popped popcorn wafted upstairs. What torture! Inhaling deeply, Amelia Bedelia pushed her face against the spindles until . . . *POP!* Her entire head went through!

Amelia Bedelia yanked her head back. *YEOW!* Her ears were caught. Her mom was right again. Her ears *were* too big for her own good.

She could hear her parents clearly now, but she couldn't pay attention. She was

too busy twisting and turning her head and trying to pull it out from between the spindles. No luck. She heard her name and something about golf.

Then Amelia Bedelia heard her father say, "I've got an early tee time. Let's hit the sack."

Before Amelia Bedelia could wonder why her father was going to a tea party and punching a bag, her parents began turning off lights. *Yipes,* she thought. *They're coming upstairs!*

Her parents would see her head protruding from the stairway like that stuffed deer head decorating the family room in

her friend Roger's house.

Amelia Bedelia was so desperate that she did a really gross thing. She spit on her fingers and then rubbed the spit behind her ears to make them slick. Then she steadily pulled her head back until . . . *POP!* Freedom!

As the lights went out in the kitchen, Amelia Bedelia scrambled down the hall and jumped back into bed. She dove under the covers and shut her eyes.

Seconds later her parents tiptoed into her room and stood right next to her bed.

Her dad leaned down to kiss her good-night and his hand brushed her ear. Then he felt her other ear.

"Hey, honey," he whispered, "Amelia Bedelia's ears feel hot."

"Hmmmm," said her mother as she pushed the hair off Amelia Bedelia's

forehead, then gently touched her ears. "No fever, but we were talking about her, so now her ears are burning."

Amelia Bedelia didn't say a word. After her parents left quietly, she and her fiery ears kept pretending to be asleep until at last she was.

Chapter 4

# Hole in None

Amelia Bedelia hoped she was having a nightmare. If this were a nightmare, she knew she could open her eyes and it would be over. But no, it was much worse. This was reality. Her father was waking her up way too early on a Saturday morning.

"Rise and shine,

sleepyhead!" said Amelia Bedelia's father.
"We've got a date with a golf course!"

Amelia Bedelia rubbed her eyes. Both
her parents were in her room.

"We're going to play golf," said her
father. "Actually, you'll get to watch me
play golf, you lucky girl."

"I'd rather watch paint drying,"
said Amelia Bedelia.

"Don't be cranky, sweetie," said her mother. "You'll get outside, walk around, get some exercise. . . ."

"Hurry and get dressed," said her dad. "Tee time is eight o'clock."

On the way to the golf course, Amelia Bedelia's father told her all about the history of golf. The game began in Scotland, so Amelia Bedelia figured that was why they'd have tea first.

They parked their car at the course and picked out a snazzy golf cart.

"Climb in," said her father.

"Dad," said Amelia Bedelia. "Aren't we supposed to walk . . . you know, exercise?"

Her father looked around, then whispered, "Don't tell Mom and I'll let you drive."

"Deal," said Amelia Bedelia, jumping in beside him.

They drove to a small hill, stopped the cart, and got out.

"I'm thirsty," said Amelia Bedelia. "Is it tea time yet?"

"There's a bag of tees right there," said her father. "Help yourself, and hand me one."

Amelia picked up the bag. She didn't see any tea, just pointy little pieces of colored wood. She handed a red one to her dad. He stuck it in the ground and balanced his golf ball on top of it.

"Golf lesson number one," said her father. "You have to address the ball."

"Address the ball?" said Amelia Bedelia. "Are we mailing it somewhere?"

"No, silly," said her father. "Just stand like this, then you can address it properly. . . ."

Amelia Bedelia stood just like her dad. Then she bent down to

35

the ball. Using her most polite, grown-up voice, she said, "Hello, Mister Ball. Are you ready to play a little golf today?"

Next, Amelia Bedelia's father demonstrated how to swing the club he called his driver. Amelia Bedelia thought this was weird. Wasn't *she* his driver? Then he hit the ball for real— *WHACK*—

and sent it flying into the air, far, far away.

"Wow!" said Amelia Bedelia. "What were you aiming for?"

"The green," said her father.

Amelia Bedelia turned in a complete circle. "But everything around us is green," she said. "The grass, bushes, trees . . ."

"See that tiny patch of grass?" her father asked, pointing into the distance.

"With the little flag on a stick?" asked Amelia Bedelia.

"Yup," he said. "That's the first hole. Now it's your turn to drive."

They hopped back into the cart. "Hang on, Dad!" said Amelia Bedelia as they sped away.

She drove them to the ball he had just hit. Driving was fun, but they were still a long way from that flag.

"Please hand me a wood," said Amelia Bedelia's father.

Amelia Bedelia looked around for a stick or a branch.

"On second thought," he said, "hand me an iron."

"You don't need one," she said. "Your clothes look fine. They're not wrinkly."

"This is an iron in golf," her father said, reaching for a club with a metal head. He used it to hit the ball again and again. And again. Each time they got closer to the green and the flag.

Amelia Bedelia followed her father in the cart, occasionally doing big loop de loops.

At last he announced, "I'm going to chip the ball now."

Amelia Bedelia was certain that a chipped ball didn't roll as well as a perfectly round ball. They'd done an experiment about this in science. He

LOW

must not have chipped the ball much, because it landed on the green and rolled smoothly toward the little hole with the flag poking out of it.

Her dad got out his putter and walked up to the ball. "When I hit the ball," he said, "pull out the pin."

"What pin?" said Amelia Bedelia. "A safety pin? A rolling pin?"

"No," said her father. "In golf, the pin is the flag. Pull the flag out of the hole."

He tapped the ball. It began rolling downhill, picking up speed and curving perfectly toward the flag. Amelia Bedelia pulled out the flag and put her foot in front of the hole. The ball bounced off her shoe.

"What did you do that for?" yelled her father.

"To keep the ball from falling into the hole," said Amelia Bedelia. "You're welcome!"

"That's the point of golf," he said. "That hole is the cup!"

"If that's the cup," said Amelia Bedelia, "you can forget about teatime. I'm not thirsty anymore."

Amelia Bedelia was glad her father only played nine holes. The last one was a water hole, where the ball had to be hit over a pond. And there were no refreshments, unless you counted the

slimy green pond, which she did not.

Her father was about to hit the ball when Amelia Bedelia noticed something. "Hey, Dad," she said, "that ball you're using looks disgusting!"

Her dad explained that he often hit the ball into the pond and lost it there.

"I've lost more balls than I can count in that pond," her father said. "That's why I'm using this yucky old one. I won't miss it if I lose it."

He was swinging his club when

WHACK!

Amelia Bedelia got an idea.

"Wait!" she hollered.

She was too late. The ball sailed away.

"Amelia Bedelia," her father said sternly. "Never interrupt an athlete who is hitting or throwing or catching a ball. It's an important rule of good sportsmanship. I didn't even see where my ball went."

He teed up another one and hit it onto the green. Amelia Bedelia wanted to go wading into the pond after his ball, but now it didn't matter. On his second putt, the ball fell into the cup. When Amelia Bedelia reached in to pull it out, she made a discovery.

"Hey," she said. "There was already a ball in here!"

She held it up for him to see, and they both recognized it. It was the beat-up ball

he had hit first. Amelia Bedelia's father looked stunned. Then he waved his putter around and threw his hat in the air. She had never seen him so mad. Then she realized he was happy. Really, really happy.

"Yippee—a hole in one!" he yelled, dancing around the cup. "I got a hole in one!"

*What a wild tea party!* thought Amelia Bedelia.

## Chapter 5

# Downward-Facing Finally

On Sunday afternoon, Amelia Bedelia found her mother practicing yoga in the guest bedroom. She looked so calm and so serene. It was relaxing just watching her. A few minutes later, Finally came in and lay down next to Amelia Bedelia's mother on the floor.

"What do you like about yoga?" asked Amelia Bedelia.

"It keeps me in shape," said her mother.

"How do you change shape?" Amelia Bedelia asked. "What shape are you now?"

Her mother was down on her hands and knees with her back straight. "This is called table pose," she said.

"I get it," said Amelia Bedelia. "Your back is the top of the table, and your legs are the legs of the table."

"My arms are legs too," said her mother, arching her back up into the air. "Now what do I look like?"

 Amelia Bedelia shrugged.

"Like a croquet hoop."

"This is cat pose," said her mother.

"Shhhh!" said Amelia Bedelia. "Don't say that word in front of Finally!"

"Here's one for her," said Amelia

Bedelia's mother as she straightened her legs and put her bottom up in the air until she looked like an upside-down letter V. "This pose is called downward-facing dog. Try it."

Amelia Bedelia got down on the floor and tried the pose. Finally stood up and

stretched the same way, poking her furry rear end high in the air.

Amelia Bedelia and her mother looked at Finally, then at each other.

"Finally does a better downward-facing dog pose than either of us," said her mother.

"Woof!" agreed Amelia Bedelia.

They began giggling and couldn't stop. Finally started to bark. She ran under their bellies, like a ball zipping through a pair of croquet hoops, until Amelia Bedelia and her mom collapsed on the floor together.

As her mother rolled up her yoga mat,

she said, "Thank you for going with your dad to play golf, sweetie. It meant a lot to him that you saw him get that hole in one."

"It was fun," said Amelia Bedelia. "I learned new words."

Her mother stopped smiling. "New words?" she asked. "What new words?"

Amelia Bedelia could tell that her mom was trying to keep a calm yoga voice.

"Golf words," said Amelia Bedelia. "Like the word 'hook.' It's not like a fishhook. It's when you hit the ball and it curves back to the left and gets lost in the bushes. Then he had a slice."

oops! Hook!

"Pizza?" asked her mother.

"Nope," said Amelia Bedelia. "This

slice is when you hit the ball and it veers to the right and bounces off a tree."

"I see," said her mother. "What happens when your dad hits the ball and it goes straight down the middle?"

Amelia Bedelia smiled and said, "He hollers 'Hooray!' and jumps in the air."

Her mother laughed.

"Hey," said Amelia Bedelia. "Where is Dad?"

"It's Sunday afternoon, cupcake," said Amelia Bedelia's mother with an exaggerated shrug. "I wonder where on earth your father could be. . . ."

Amelia Bedelia understood immediately.

## Chapter 6

# Get the Cents Back

Amelia Bedelia went downstairs to the
family room. Her father was snug
as a bug in his recliner. He
was eating chips and dip and
watching football.

Amelia Bedelia sat on the footstool. She did her best to look interested in the game, which was just beginning. Football had always baffled her, but her dad loved it, so she was open to giving it another try.

"Why is that guy dressed like a zebra?" she asked, pointing at the man in a black-and-white-striped shirt.

"That's the ref—the referee," said her father. "He makes sure the players follow the rules. See, he just flipped a quarter to decide which team will kick the ball to the other team."

"Who are those two other guys on the field with him, the ones wearing numbers?" asked Amelia Bedelia.

"They're quarterbacks," said her dad.

"Did Zebra Guy give them back their quarters?" asked Amelia Bedelia.

"No," said her father. "Each team tries to get the other team's quarterback."

Amelia Bedelia was amazed. "Do you mean those guys knock into one another just trying to get a quarter back?"

Her dad laughed. "Those guys get paid millions of dollars to tackle one another," he said.

"That's a lot of quarters," said Amelia Bedelia, dipping a chip into the dip. Once the game began,

56

Amelia Bedelia's father acted as though he was playing too.

He yelled at the TV, telling the players where to run, when to pass, and how to tackle. He spent every minute cheering and booing and even jumping in the air and grabbing his hair.

"Maybe you ought to play football instead of golf, Dad," said Amelia Bedelia.

Her father was not listening. "Uh-oh," he said. "Our quarterback is behind the eight ball."

*Gosh,* thought Amelia Bedelia, *even the ball has a number.* No wonder she was clueless when it came to football! It was all about math. There were scores and

$\div\ 4\ =\ ?$

penalties and measurements involved. Football players were covered in numbers, and some players were even fractions. She could hear Mrs. Robbins now: "If a quarterback has the number twelve on his uniform, and you divide that by four, what number is he really? If a halfback

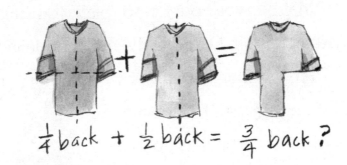

$\frac{1}{4}$ back $+$ $\frac{1}{2}$ back $=$ $\frac{3}{4}$ back ?

has the number twenty on his uniform, is he really a ten or a five?"

Amelia Bedelia discovered that the game itself was divided into quarters.

At halftime she and her dad watched a band marching around the field in fancy geometric formations. Worse still, the announcers kept talking about numbers called statistics, measuring how these teams were doing compared to other teams and past games. Numbers kept pouring off the screen, flowing out of the speakers, flooding the family room with a tidal wave of math that left her floating on her footstool in a sea of arithmetic. Thank

 goodness for the yummy chips and dip!

Then Amelia Bedelia heard a sound that was music to her ears.

"Z-z-z-z-z-z-z-z . . ."

Her dad had fallen asleep. She gently slid the remote out of his hand. She lowered the volume so she wouldn't wake him up while she was changing the channel to something good.

Amelia Bedelia found a nature show about a troop of gorillas. They were fighting over a coconut. A silverback took it away from the others and ran off with it. Some zebras were grazing in background. It looked like a football game, without any numbers.

Just then, her dad snorted and opened his eyes groggily. His glasses fell off.

"What's the score?" he asked, squinting at the screen.

"Twenty-one to fourteen," said Amelia Bedelia, remembering the score of the football game before she switched the channel.

"Who's ahead?' he asked.

"The team with twenty-one points," she said.

"That's right," said her dad, rolling over to resume his nap. "That's how football works. *Z-z-z-z-z-z.*"

Amelia Bedelia couldn't blame him. This weekend had worn her out too. She couldn't wait to get back to school and away from sports for a while.

Zzzzz

## Chapter 7

# Marathon, Pentathlon, and On and On . . .

On Monday, Amelia Bedelia discovered one good thing about spending her Saturday on a golf course. None of the other kids in her class had ever played golf—miniature golf, maybe, but not real grown-up golf. Amelia Bedelia told everyone how she'd helped her father get a hole in one.

"Whoa," said Skip. "My dad would give anything for that."

Even Dawn was impressed. "*I'd* give anything for that!" she said.

With sports out of the way, Amelia Bedelia was ready for social studies. She loved anything to do with history, because it had already happened. There were no surprises. She loved ancient history most of all, because that stuff had happened so long ago, it was . . . well . . . ancient!

"I've got a surprise for you!" announced Mr. Tobin, their social studies teacher. "Today we start our study of ancient

Greece. We will reach back thousands of years, travel across time and space to bring those times into the present. We will learn about Greek inventions and food and families and the Greek gods and myths. We will relive those ancient  times by holding our own Greek Games, an athletic competition featuring a variety of sports from ancient Greece."

While the entire class erupted in cheers and shouts, Amelia Bedelia sat in stunned silence. She was doomed. There was no escaping sports. Sports had been around for thousands of years. Fortunately, she wasn't the only one worrying.

"What sports did

the ancient Greeks play?" asked Teddy.

"Well," said Mr. Tobin, "the first marathon was run by a Greek messenger."

"Are we running a marathon?" asked Holly.

"Certainly not," said Mr. Tobin. "A marathon is more than twenty-six miles."

"Wow," said Cliff. "That messenger must have gotten a medal."

"Actually," said Mr. Tobin, "right after he delivered the message, he died."

"Died?" said Clay. "Actually died?"

"Don't worry," said Mr. Tobin. "We're going to do an ancient pentathlon, just like they did back in 708 BC."

"I hope it's a shorter race," said Clay.

"It is," said Mr. Tobin. "Remember

your geometry—also invented
by the Greeks. A *penta*gon has
five sides. So a *penta*thlon has

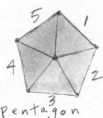

Pentagon

five events, one of which
is a short race. You'll only have to run
a hundred meters. That's about one
hundred and nine yards."

Everyone except Amelia Bedelia
breathed a sigh of relief. Some of the yards

Mrs. Adams's yard

Our yard

+ 102 more!! = 109 yards!

in her neighborhood were really big. She couldn't imagine what it would be like to run through one hundred and nine of them. She'd have to stop and rest, for sure.

"What are the other four events?" asked Angel.

Mr. Tobin turned to the blackboard and made a list. "A pentathlon includes the hundred-meter run, long jump, wrestling, discus throw, and last but not least, javelin," he said.

discus

"Javelin?" asked Clay. "We get to throw a spear?"

javelin

"You bet," said Mr. Tobin. "But we will do it safely, I assure you."

Mr. Tobin spent the rest of social studies answering questions and talking about how important sports were in ancient Greece. He showed them pictures with statues of athletes throwing a discus and a javelin. He also showed them pictures of big vases decorated with images of

discus

long jump

wrestling

footrace

javelin

athletes wrestling or jumping.

Clay raised his hand. "Mr. Tobin," he said, "those ancient athletes are naked. Can we wear clothes at our pentathlon?"

Mr. Tobin waited for the laughter to die down before he answered. "Yes, on one condition," he said. "Your assignment is to wear chitons and sandals, just like the Greek boys and girls would have done. Look, here's a picture."

Chip said, "It's a toga party!" Everyone cheered.

"Save that for the pentathlon," said Mr. Tobin. Then he showed them one last picture. It was an image of a big plate that was in a museum. Greek athletes were

← chiton

← sandals

running in a footrace around the rim of the plate. There was no starting point or finish line. It was impossible to tell who was winning and who was losing or who was ahead and who was behind. They had been chasing one another around the rim of that plate, in an endless circle, for thousands of years, just for the pure joy of running. Amelia Bedelia loved it.

If the ancient Greeks were choosing teams, would they have chosen her? Water fountains hadn't been invented yet. Would the team captain have picked an animal skin filled with cool water before choosing Amelia Bedelia?

Chapter 8

# On Your Mark, Get Set . . . STOP!

The first practice session for the pentathlon took place on an unusually hot and humid day. Amelia Bedelia and her classmates were sent out to the lower field for gym.

*TWEEEEEEET!*

Some kids jumped, and others covered their ears. Everyone spun around. A

young woman was standing before them, a clipboard in one hand and a water bottle in the other. She had a large silver whistle between her lips. She let the whistle fall and dangle from a lanyard around her neck.

"Afternoon, kids. My name is Mrs. Thompson. You may call me Mrs. Thompson or Coach Thompson, but I prefer just Coach. I usually work with the older kids, but Mr. Tobin has asked me to get you in shape for your Greek Games. Any questions?"

Rose raised her hand. "It's pretty hot. Can we sit in the shade until—"

"Nope," said Coach Thompson. "Now line up, and let's have a look at you."

Everyone shuffled into a wavy, lumpy line. They resembled an anaconda that had stuffed itself at Thanksgiving.

Coach Thompson clapped sharply

three times. "Come on, come on! Move it! Line up alphabetically," she called out.

That was easy for Amelia Bedelia. Her name put her at the head of the line. She would be the first to be inspected by Mrs. Thompson.

"Hello," said Mrs. Thompson.

"Hello, Just Coach," said Amelia Bedelia.

"What did you call me?" asked Mrs. Thompson.

"Just Coach," said Amelia Bedelia. "You said that's what you prefer."

"Not just," said Mrs. Thompson. "Only Coach."

"Okay, Only Coach," said Amelia Bedelia.

*"Coach,"* said Mrs. Thompson. "No

'only' or 'just' before it.  I'm Coach, period."

Amelia Bedelia thought about asking Coach Period why she kept changing her name, but she decided to nod instead.

Coach Period asked for her name and wrote it down on her clipboard. "Amelia Bedelia," she said.

"That's right," said Amelia Bedelia.

"That's alphabetical," said Coach Period, continuing down the line.

"Now," she said, when she had recorded everyone's name. "Running is fundamental to fitness. I want to see how fast you kids are. You're all going to run to that water fountain and back while I time you."

A shiver ran through Amelia Bedelia.

Not the water fountain again! This was a bad omen.

"Okay," said Coach Period. "The race will begin when I say, 'On your mark, get set, go!'"

Amelia Bedelia took off.

"Amelia Bedelia! Stop!" yelled the coach. *TWEEEEEET!* "Come back!"

Amelia Bedelia turned around and

TWEET!

TWEEeeeet! tweet

trotted back. She could hear snickering. She crouched down again, breathing hard.

"Haven't you ever raced before?" said Coach Period. "Wait until I say the word 'Go.'"

Amelia Bedelia took off again, sprinting even faster.

TWEEEET!!!

*TWEEEEEET!*

"Get back here, Amelia Bedelia!" hollered Coach.

Amelia Bedelia stopped and walked back to her place in line, even more out of breath. Now everyone was giggling.

Coach Period looked right at Amelia Bedelia and said, "Do not move a muscle until I say you-know-what word.

"On your mark . . . get set—"

"Coach," interrupted Cliff. "This is an emergency. I *really* need to go to the bathroom."

Coach Period turned to Cliff and hollered, "Okay, already. Go!"

Amelia Bedelia took off as fast as she could. The coach stood there dumbstruck. Then she started her stopwatch and said, "Well, what's everyone waiting for? Didn't you hear me say GO?"

The rest of the class took off together like a thundering herd. Holly came in first, as she always did. She was fast. Even with her head start, Amelia Bedelia stumbled

across the finish line in last place, as she
always did.

Coach studied her stopwatch. "Let
me tell you where you stand," she said,
shaking her head.

Amelia Bedelia looked around. No
one was standing. Everyone was walking
around puffing and panting or lying on the
ground gasping and wheezing.

"You all need a lot of conditioning," said Coach, shaking her head.

Amelia Bedelia thought everyone's hair looked great. No one needed more conditioning, especially not Angel. Amelia Bedelia wished she had hair like Angel's.

Amelia Bedelia whispered to Clay, "Do you need hair conditioning?"

"No, thanks," said Clay. "But I could use some air-conditioning."

*TWEEEET!*

"Follow me, young Greeks!" yelled Coach.

TWeeeeet!

82

Then she led them in a jog around the field—*five times* around the field!

"It's like a pentajog," said Amelia Bedelia to Rose.

"It's a nightmare," said Rose.

Coach ran ahead, but *backward*, giving them advice and encouragement until it was time to return to the classroom.

## Chapter 9

# The Hundred-Meter Dash

Mr. Tobin was drawing a picture of two winding snakes on the board when the class staggered back into the room.

"Whoa, you all look exhausted," he said. "I asked Coach not to make you guys run a marathon on your very first day of training."

"She ran us into the ground," said Joy.

"My blisters have blisters," said Heather, taking off her shoes to rub her feet.

"Phew!" said Clay. "Did a skunk pass by?"

Heather glared at him and put her shoes back on.

"Did you hear what Coach told us?" asked Skip. "She said, 'Sometimes you have to go the extra mile.' I've never run even one mile before today, and she expects me to run an extra one!"

"Tell that to that dead messenger," said Cliff. "If he had stopped at twenty-five miles instead of going for twenty-six, he might still be alive today."

Cliff and Skip laughed.

"That's so dumb," said Penny. "He lived and died thousands of years ago. You make it sound like you could see him jogging in the park right this minute."

"Yeah, don't listen to Cliff," said Wade. "He totally missed the first race. When the going got tough, Cliff was going to the bathroom!"

"Oh, yeah?" said Cliff. He tackled Wade, and they rolled on the ground.

"Break it up, guys," said Mr. Tobin. "Save that for the wrestling ring at the Greek Games, shall we? Before we learn what it was like to live in ancient Greece, I'll make a deal with you. I'm willing to forget about assigning homework for a few days if you'll use the extra time to do sports

86

homework—go jogging, play games, and get more exercise."

"You're giving us a vacation from homework?" said Clay.

"Let's call it a homework hiatus," said Mr. Tobin.

"My uncle had an operation to repair his hiatus," said Pat. "He's fine now."

Amelia Bedelia knew that Pat couldn't be right because of the way Penny was rolling her eyes. Penny was going to be a doctor, so she knew more than anyone in class about the human body. Also, it was clear that Mr. Tobin was trying really hard not to laugh.

"Thank you for sharing some family history, Pat," said Mr. Tobin, smiling.

"Let's talk about medicine and the ancient Greeks. The Greeks were some of the first doctors the world had known. Hippocrates is considered the father of medicine, founding the first medical school around 400 BC. And we get our symbol for medicine from a Greek god."

Amelia Bedelia saw Penny perk up and start taking notes. Like Penny, she was really interested in what Mr. Tobin was saying. But her eyes kept straying to the list that was still on the board, the five events of the pentathlon. She had never thrown a discus, and her parents probably weren't going to let her toss a javelin around

TODAY IS
400 B

FIRST DOCTOR'S
APPOINTMENT

88

their backyard. But she could certainly practice the hundred-meter dash. In fact, she knew exactly where she could find at least a hundred meters in a row.

After school, Amelia Bedelia dropped her backpack at home, ate  a quick snack with Finally, and explained her sports homework to her mom. Then she jogged downtown.

Main Street was several blocks long, with parking meters on both sides. She counted thirty-one on one side of the street and twenty-nine on the other side. The numbers weren't equal because there were two driveways on the twenty-nine

side, where people couldn't park. She found the other forty meters she needed on two side streets.

Now came the tricky part. She had to time herself so she would arrive at the crosswalk just as the light changed. That way the cars would be stopped and the WALK sign lit up, and she would be able to cross safely. Phew! Running was complicated. Did the ancient

Greeks have to deal with  this?

On her first try, she got past the thirty-one meters but had to wait at the light. On her next attempt, the crosswalk sign was flashing DON'T WALK. She ran in place until she realized that she was not walking—she was *running*. So she sprinted across the street before the light changed.

Amelia Bedelia was counting off the next set of meters—thirty-two, thirty-three, thirty-four, thirty-five—when she heard a sound that brought her to a screeching halt.

*TWEEEEET!*

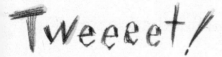

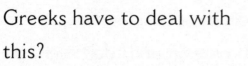

Oh, no! Coach Period must have tracked her down! Turning around took every bit of courage Amelia Bedelia could muster. Uh-oh! It wasn't Coach Period. It was way worse. It was Officer O'Brien!

Amelia Bedelia really hoped the policeman didn't remember her. She'd had a run-in with him in the park after picking a flower bed clean and then selling the bouquet for twenty dollars. But that was another story.

"What's going on?" said Officer O'Brien. "Did someone tell you to go play in traffic?"

"No, sir," said Amelia Bedelia. "I'm running a hundred meters for homework."

Officer O'Brien looked down the row of meters, smiled, and said, "There's a big difference between a hundred meters and a hundred parking meters." He paced off the distance between two parking meters. "That's about twenty feet." He wrote TWENTY FEET on the sidewalk with the chalk he used to mark the tires of parked cars.

"If you multiply twenty feet by one hundred parking meters, you get 2,000 feet. But one hundred meters (the distance) is only about 330 feet. So when you run past a hundred parking meters, how much extra have you run?"

Officer O'Brien handed his chalk to Amelia Bedelia. She wondered if he was

$$2{,}000 - 330$$

friends with Mrs. Robbins. They could do math together. She wrote 330 under the 2,000 and subtracted it.

"Hey," said Amelia Bedelia. "I ran 1,670 feet too far."

The policeman nodded. "If I were you," he said, "I'd set up a course 330 feet long in your neighborhood. And Amelia

Bedelia," he added, "when 'Don't Walk' is flashing, that doesn't mean dash across the street before the light changes. 'Don't Walk' means stop."

"Thanks, Officer O'Brien," she said.

Then Officer O'Brien picked a flower from a nearby planter. "Take this to your mother," he said, smiling.

Amelia Bedelia was relieved that her only problem with Officer O'Brien had been a math problem.

## Chapter 10

# Throw like a Girl, Shake like a Boy

Amelia Bedelia set up a running course as soon as she got home. Finally raced along beside her, and she wished she could run as fast as her dog. That's the only chance she'd have of beating anyone, especially Holly, who was faster than every girl *and* boy in the class.

Amelia Bedelia practiced her

hundred-meter dash every day that week. But how, she wondered, would she ever learn to wrestle? At a time like this, an older brother or sister would come in handy. Even a younger brother or sister would help.

She'd asked her parents for a baby brother or sister. She'd gotten her own dog instead. So she decided that Finally was going to be her wrestling partner. After all, Amelia Bedelia's favorite parts of nature shows were the wrestling matches between the young animals. She loved to watch lion cubs shoving each other around or a pair of bear

cubs squabbling over honey. They were so cute!

Finally was taking a nap. Amelia Bedelia got down on her knees and snuck up behind her. She grabbed Finally's favorite chew toy, a blue plastic duck. Finally opened one eye.

"Come get it!" Amelia Bedelia teased.

Finally latched on to the duck and away they went, tugging back and forth,

up and down, from side to side, then rolling around on the ground together. Finally loved helping Amelia Bedelia with her homework.

Finally did teach Amelia Bedelia one move. They were both tugging at the toy, straining with all their might, when Finally suddenly let go. Amelia Bedelia went tumbling backward. She dropped the duck in surprise. Finally scooped it up,

her tail wagging in triumph.

"Smart girl!" said Amelia
Bedelia. "Want to go for a walk?"

It was a gorgeous day, so the
park was packed with people and dogs
enjoying the weather. "Hi, Amelia
Bedelia!" said Diana. She was walking a
bunch of dogs with her boyfriend, Eric.

"We just saw Charlie walking Pierre."

Amelia Bedelia had once helped Diana with her dog-walking service, and Eric had helped Amelia Bedelia and her friend Charlie solve a poodle problem. Maybe Eric could help her again.

"Hey, Eric," said Amelia Bedelia. "Do you know how to throw a javelin?"

Eric laughed, but Diana laughed louder. "Well," said Eric, "I was in the military a while ago, but not *that* long ago. Why do you want to throw a javelin?"

Amelia Bedelia told them all about the upcoming pentathlon and how Finally was helping her learn to wrestle.

"I once took a self-defense course," said Diana. "I'll show you what I know."

Eric held the leashes while Diana and Amelia Bedelia headed to a grassy spot.

"If you have to wrestle someone bigger or stronger," said Diana, "you can use their size and strength against them."

She showed Amelia Bedelia how to push against opponents and then pull them off balance. It was the same move that Finally had taught her.

"Remember," said Diana as she and Eric headed off to deliver the dogs to

their owners. "Always stand tall!"

"Thanks for helping me!" yelled Amelia Bedelia.

Just then Amelia Bedelia spotted Charlie. Actually, Pierre saw Finally first and came running to greet them with a tennis ball in his mouth. Pierre dropped the ball at Amelia Bedelia's feet.

"Hi, Charlie," said Amelia Bedelia.

"Hey, Amelia Bedelia!" said Charlie. "Looks like Pierre wants you to throw the ball for him."

Amelia Bedelia picked up the ball and threw it with all her might. It soared through the air for about ten feet before it landed on the ground,

bounced once, and rolled a couple of feet more.

Pierre looked at the ball, then back at Amelia Bedelia. He had a funny look on his furry face that said, That's the best you can do? Even Finally looked embarrassed.

"Hah," Charlie blurted out. "You throw like a girl!"

Amelia Bedelia's face turned bright red. She felt angry and ashamed and confused and uncomfortable all at once.

"That's right, Charlie," said Amelia

Bedelia. "I throw like a girl, because I *am* a girl. And so is Finally. Which is just fine. But since you have a problem with that, we're leaving!"

Charlie caught up with her and grabbed her arm. She was tempted to use one of

her new wrestling moves on him, but he was already apologizing.

"Amelia Bedelia," he said, "I'm sorry.

I'm just surprised you don't know the secret of throwing."

"What secret?" asked Amelia Bedelia, blinking away her tears.

Charlie showed her how gripping the ball with two fingers gives it a spin that keeps it on track to where it's aimed. "Use your whole body," he said, "not just your arm. Plus, take a few steps so you get the energy from your legs too."

Charlie helped her with each move until she had it down. "Now here's the secret," he said, almost in a whisper. "Cross your right leg over your left on the last

step. When you untwist, all the power of your body goes into the throw, like this."

Charlie gripped the ball, jogged a few steps, twisted his right leg over his left,

and rocketed the ball into the air.

Pierre and Finally looked at each other, then went racing off to retrieve it.

"Wow!" said Amelia Bedelia. "That's great!"

When the dogs came

back with the ball, Amelia Bedelia wiped the puppy  spit off it and tried Charlie's secret method. It worked! She'd never thrown that far before. "Wow!" she hollered, jumping into the air.

"We're friends again, right?" asked Charlie, holding out his hand.

"I'll always be your friend," said Amelia Bedelia. "Even though you shake hands like a boy."

They laughed, parting ways, their dogs leading them home. Amelia Bedelia's mother was waiting on the front steps, holding what used to be her best cake pans.

Eeew! Dog slobber!!

108

## Chapter 11

# Greece-y Pan Quakes

Amelia Bedelia's mother was holding a pan in each hand, waving them around like those workers at the airport who direct planes to their parking spots.

"Young lady," said her mother. "What did you do to my cake pans?"

"It was for homework," said Amelia Bedelia. "Rose and Daisy and I needed something shaped like a discus so we could practice our throwing."

"You threw my baking pans around the yard?" asked Amelia Bedelia's mother.

"Mom, they're made of metal," said Amelia Bedelia. "They didn't break."

"They're dented," said her mother. "Here comes your father. Let's see what he has to say."

Amelia Bedelia's father had heard

them arguing a block away. He walked up to his house with all the enthusiasm of someone headed over a cliff.

"What are you two up to?" he asked.

"I'm up to four feet and one inch," said Amelia Bedelia. "Mom is probably the same height she was when you left this morning."

"But I've had it up to here with these

Greek Games," said her mother, indicating a level just above her head. "Look at my cake pans."

"Amelia Bedelia will have to pay for new pans," said her father.

"I need them tonight," said Amelia Bedelia's mother. "I'm baking cakes for the class picnic after the pentathlon."

"Besides dented discus cakes," he asked, "what else is on the menu? I hope the food isn't Greece-y."

Amelia Bedelia and her mother groaned.

"Daaad," said Amelia Bedelia.

"Then you should love what we're having tonight," said Amelia Bedelia's mother. "We're eating vegetarian."

Amelia Bedelia's father made a

face. "I've never gotten used to eating vegetarians," he said. "Those folks taste like broccoli that's gone bad."

"Daaad . . ." A shiver ran down Amelia Bedelia's spine. "Don't say that," she said. "I will totally lose my appetite."

"Sorry, cupcake. Let's feast on rabbit food," he said, clapping his hands and rubbing them together with fake excitement.

"Honey, I did make you a couch potato," said Amelia Bedelia's mother.

That was his favorite—a double-stuffed baked potato with two kinds of cheese.

"Gangway!" he said, running up the steps. Zzzz

## Chapter 12

# High Pentas All Around

The next day was the day of the Greek Games. Mr. Tobin, Coach, and everyone in Amelia Bedelia's class arrived at school dressed in chitons or tunics and sandals. Amelia Bedelia and some of her friends even fixed their hair in ancient hairstyles. For fun, they posed like the Greeks pictured on ancient vases and pottery.

When it was time for the pentathlon to begin, they traded in their sandals for sneakers. The class paraded outside, carrying flags and banners representing the five events of the pentathlon. They marched down to the lower field, where parents and some of the younger kids at their school had already gathered, cheering, to watch the games.

The first event was the discus.

"You'll get two chances to throw the discus," said Coach. "I'll record every throw, and we will officially mark on the field the two longest throws made."

Amelia Bedelia was tenth in line. Her first throw was okay. It wasn't the longest throw, and it wasn't the shortest. It was right in the middle. Then she spotted her

mother in the crowd. Amelia Bedelia
wanted to show her mom that she had
wrecked her cake pans for an important

reason. She whirled around once, twice,
three times. She kept whirling around and
around like a tornado.

"Let go, already!" shouted Coach.

Amelia Bedelia did, and the discus
went flying up, up, up in a high arc. Then

it came down and struck the ground. It was the longest throw so far. But instead of being happy, Amelia Bedelia was so dizzy that she staggered three steps and fell over, the sky spinning above her. Her mother ran over to make sure she was all right.

"Great throw, sweetheart," whispered her mom as she helped Amelia Bedelia to her feet. "I'm glad my cake pans paid off."

Amelia Bedelia's toss was the longest until Pat threw the discus. Both of his throws were longer than Amelia Bedelia's, so Pat got first place and Amelia Bedelia came in second.

"The most important part of playing

sports is being a good sport," said Mr. Tobin. "That's why we are now going to perform that traditional sporting salute of ancient Greece, the high penta."

Mr. Tobin turned to Pat and gave him a high five. The rest of the class followed suit.

"Nice win, Pat!" said Coach, smiling.

Amelia Bedelia was tired already, and she was not ready for the hundred-meter dash, which was the next event. She was thinking about "pulling a Cliff" and heading to the restroom. She could really use a rest! But her classmates were assembling on the starting line, so she did too. There was the finish line, marked with white tape, just a hundred meters away. She could do it! They all crouched down, ready for the signal.

"On your marks . . . get set . . . GO!"

Holly took the lead right away, with Wade, Teddy, and Dawn hot on her heels, followed by Amelia Bedelia. Then it happened. Wade tripped and fell, causing Teddy and Dawn to tumble down too. Amelia Bedelia jumped over the tangled bunch and kept running. Then Suzanne fell on the pile and a bunch of other kids stumbled too. Holly looked back over her shoulder to see

what the commotion was, and that cost her dearly.

Amelia Bedelia was coming up fast, huffing and puffing. "Slow down, Holly! Slow down, Holly!"

"No way," said Holly as Amelia Bedelia drew alongside her. They were both heading for the finish line, neck and neck. Holly suddenly leaned as far forward as she could, almost falling on her face—but breaking the tape at the finish line before Amelia Bedelia.

"Holly wins by a nose!" shouted Mr. Tobin, who was right there watching.

The crowd went wild!

Amelia Bedelia stretched out her leg muscles as the rest of the class staggered

and limped across the line. She didn't feel that bad. It wasn't that she wasn't fast enough. Her real problem was that her nose was too short.

On her way to the water fountain for a drink, Amelia Bedelia gave Holly a high

penta with each hand. "Congratulations," she said.

"Our first high deca!" said Mr. Tobin. "What an honor!"

The next event, the javelin throw, let everyone catch their breath. Coach and Mr. Tobin cleared the field. Some parents, including Amelia Bedelia's father, stood guard, making sure that no

one got hurt. "We don't want any student shish kebobs," he said.

As with the discus toss, each student got two throws. Using Charlie's right-leg-across-left secret throwing technique, Amelia Bedelia threw the javelin farther than any girl and almost any boy. Only Clay hurled it farther down the field. There were high pentas for him, and another second place for Amelia Bedelia.

## Chapter 13

# A Lonnnnnggg Jump to a Short End

Amelia Bedelia hadn't practiced her long jump, except in gym class. As it turned out, she didn't need to. She went running toward the white board where you take off, building up speed before she leaped into the air. As she took off, she heard Coach cry out, "Scratch!"

Amelia Bedelia touched down in the

landing pit. Her arms were windmilling to help her keep her balance, but she couldn't stay upright, and she fell back into the soft sand.

"Sorry," said Mr. Tobin as he measured her jump. "Because you fell backward, I have to measure from where your body hit the sand, not your feet."

Amelia Bedelia jogged back to the

starting block for her next try. When she got there, Coach gave her more bad news.

"You scratched," said Coach.

"Scratched what?" asked Amelia Bedelia. She didn't remember having an itch. Oh, maybe she had scratched some equipment when she took off!

"Your toe slipped over the line before you jumped," said Coach. "I had to disqualify your first attempt. In sports, that's called a 'scratch.' You've got one more try."

Now Amelia Bedelia was nervous. She wasn't worried about winning. She was having too much fun coming in second time after time. She had a runner-up reputation to uphold!

Amelia Bedelia started to run, picking

*scratch!*

up speed, going faster and faster, but making sure that she didn't go over the line again. She was just about to take off when . . . *TWEEEEEEET!*

"EEEHHH—*YAHHHHHHH!*" screamed Amelia Bedelia.

A blowing whistle always made her jump. She flew into the air, her arms and legs spinning around and around, her feet still running. She soared up and up, flying straight toward Mr. Tobin. She landed far into the pit. Like before, her whole body

began teeter-tottering, knees going in and out, arms swinging back and forth. She struggled against gravity to keep from falling backward.

Mr. Tobin made big scooping motions with his arms. "Come on, Amelia Bedelia!" he hollered. "Fall toward me."

She leaned forward and hit the sand.

"I've never been so happy to fall on my face," she said as Mr. Tobin measured her jump and the crowd cheered.

"Congratulations," he said. "Your jump put you in first place!"

"Amelia Bedelia!" shouted Coach. "Great jump! Sorry about the whistle! We had a situation."

Amelia Bedelia waved and smiled. She felt funny in first, after being second so many times. She didn't get to feel funny for long. Skip bested her best by two inches, just the length of one of her mother's yummy brownies! So Amelia Bedelia came in second for the fourth time in a row.

The real surprise came in the fifth and final event—wrestling. Who knew that Amelia Bedelia would be such a star? She won match after match! The final match of the

pentathlon pitted her against her friend Angel, who was the sweetest and kindest person she knew. Amelia Bedelia was almost positive she would beat Angel.

She didn't want to, but if she pretended they were ancient Greek girls, it wouldn't be so bad. She wished Angel good luck and planted her feet.

"Thanks," said Angel. "I hope you win, Amelia Bedelia."

Coach blew her whistle to start the final match. In seconds, Angel was all over Amelia Bedelia. Slipping behind

her in a flash, Angel wrapped her arms around Amelia Bedelia, pinning both of Amelia Bedelia's arms while using a leg to sweep her off her feet. BOOM! Down went Amelia Bedelia, with Angel on top.

*TWEET!*

Coach raised Angel's arm in triumph. The match was over! Already?

"Wow!" said Amelia Bedelia. "That was amazing!" She gave Angel a high penta and a hug.

Amelia Bedelia was second again!

Chapter 14

# When Second Comes First

Mr. Tobin thanked everyone for participating in the Greek Games—the students for their enthusiasm, and the parents and other teachers for their support, especially Coach Thompson, who got a big round of applause.

Mr. Tobin went on, "As my good friend Aristotle said, 'A body capable of enduring

all efforts, either of the racecourse or of
bodily strength . . . is why the athletes in
the pentathlon are most beautiful.' Thank
you all for making this such a beautiful and
fun day at our school."

Parents clapped loudly, and the
students cheered.

"Our winners today will be awarded
the highest honor in ancient Greece, a
wreath of laurel leaves to wear on their

heads as a symbol of their victory."

Mr. Tobin and Coach stood at the front, holding six wreaths.

*Five events = five winners, which does not = six wreaths,* thought Amelia Bedelia.

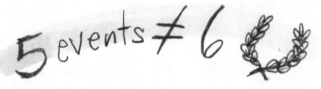

These Greek Games were not adding up.

Mr. Tobin called the winners to come forward. He announced the winners' names, the events they had won, and their winning time or distance. Then Coach placed a wreath on each winner's head, and they all shook hands. When the fifth one had been presented, Mr. Tobin held up one last wreath.

"This is an extra wreath," he said. "It was made by mistake, but now I think it was not a mistake at all. One athlete among you never knew the thrill of coming in first. Second place was as close as she came. But that student did it five times. Let me tell you, being in second place five times adds up to being the best all-around athlete in our class. Where is Amelia Bedelia?"

Amelia Bedelia had been in the back, but now a path cleared for her to come forward. Mr. Tobin handed the wreath to Coach, who placed it on Amelia Bedelia's head. Then she said, "You worked hard to make yourself stronger and faster. Even though you didn't win any events, you always cheered your classmates on. You

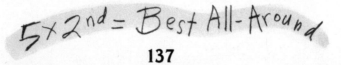
5 × 2nd = Best All-Around

captured the spirit of good sportsmanship, born in ancient Greece, and helped make these Greek Games a success."

Everyone was clapping loudly, cheering and stomping their feet.

"I declare these Greek Games over," said Mr. Tobin. "Let's eat!"

Everyone enjoyed a picnic lunch on colorful blankets on the grass where minutes before they had been throwing,

racing, tossing, jumping, and wrestling. Mr. Tobin and Coach came by to thank Amelia Bedelia's mother for her delicious honey cake.

"We both took huge slices," said Coach.

"Yes," said Mr. Tobin. "We put a dent in it."

"It was dented from the start," said Amelia Bedelia's mother.

"Put your laurel wreath back on, sweetie," said Amelia Bedelia's father. "I want to get a picture of you with Mr. Tobin and Coach Thompson."

Amelia Bedelia touched the top of her head, but her wreath was gone. How could she have lost it, after all she went through to win it?

"There it is," said her mother. "You're sitting on it."

"Aha!" said Mr. Tobin. "Are you resting on your laurels already, Amelia Bedelia?"

She put her wreath back on her head, and her dad took a picture that ended up in the school newspaper.

On their way home, Amelia Bedelia's father leaned over and said to his wife,

"Honey, at our next parent meeting with Mr. Tobin, remind me to suggest a celebration of golf. I could volunteer and show the kids how to putt and—"

"Drive golf carts?" asked Amelia Bedelia.

"Not your father," said Amelia Bedelia's mother. "He only golfs for the exercise."

Amelia Bedelia and her dad winked at each other in the rearview mirror.

"I know we just came from a picnic," he said. "But I could use a bite to eat right now."

"Me too," said Amelia Bedelia. "I'm starving after all that exercise."

Amelia Bedelia's mother made a suggestion. "We could get french fries at Pete's Diner."

"Pete's is nice," said Amelia Bedelia's father. "But I was hoping to work on my slice."

Amelia Bedelia's mother shook her head. "Golf!" she said. "Is golf the only thing you think about?"

"Of course not," said Amelia Bedelia's father. "I was thinking that we could go to Perfect Pizza, and then I'll work on a slice with pepperoni and a slice with sausage and a slice with extra cheese." And that is exactly what they did.

# Two Ways to Say It

### By Amelia Bedelia

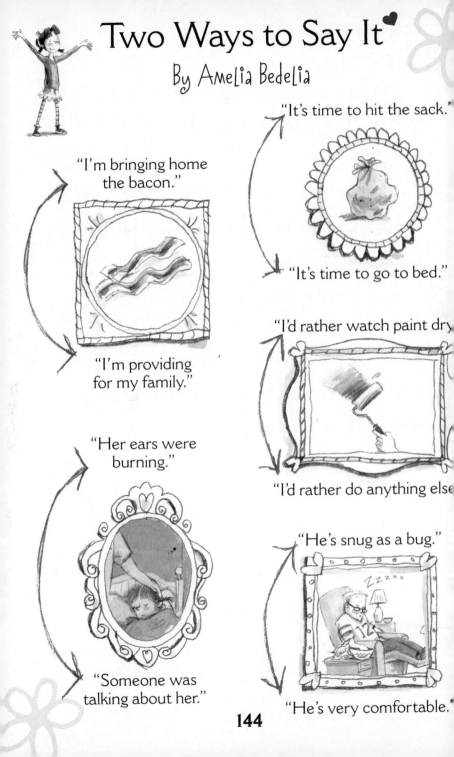

"I'm bringing home the bacon."

"I'm providing for my family."

"Her ears were burning."

"Someone was talking about her."

"It's time to hit the sack."

"It's time to go to bed."

"I'd rather watch paint dry."

"I'd rather do anything else."

"He's snug as a bug."

"He's very comfortable."

144

"My dad is a couch potato."

"My dad likes to sit around relaxing."

"She won by a nose."

"She barely beat the other person."

"Stand tall!"

"Be strong and proud of yourself!"

"You are a good sport."

"You are fair and agreeable."

"Don't rest on your laurels!"

"Keep trying and working hard, even though you've already done so many great things!"

# The Amelia Bedelia Chapter Books
## Have you read them all?

Coming
soon!

Coming
soon!

Amelia Bedelia wants a new bike—a brand-new shiny, beautiful, fast bike just like Suzanne's new bike. Amelia Bedelia's dad says that a bike like that is really expensive and will cost an arm and a leg. Amelia Bedelia doesn't want to give away one of her arms and one of her legs. She'll need both arms to steer her new bike, and both legs to pedal it.

KEEP OFF the GRASS

Amelia Bedelia is going to get a puppy—a sweet, adorable, loyal, friendly puppy! When Amelia Bedelia's parents ask her what kind of dog she'd like, Amelia Bedelia doesn't know what to say. There are hundreds and thousands of dogs in the world, maybe even millions!

#2

Amelia Bedelia is hitting the road. Where is she going? It's a surprise! But one thing is certain. Amelia Bedelia and her mom and dad will try new things (like fishing), they'll eat a lot of pizza (yum), and Amelia Bedelia will meet a new friend—a friend she'll never, *ever* forget.

Amelia Bedelia has an amazing idea! She is going to design and build a zoo in her backyard. Better yet, she is going to invite all her friends to bring their pets and help plan the exhibits and rides.

#4

**#7 Coming soon!**

**#8 Coming soon!**

Time for vacation! Amelia Bedelia is having fun with her cousin at the beach. But who is that kid they see everywhere they go?

Amelia Bedelia loves to dance, but she's not sure ballet is for her. Everyone pitches in to help her keep her toes tapping, in this silly story about dancing and performing on the big stage.

# Meet Amelia Bedelia and her friends!

# Meet Amelia Bedelia

## The 10 best things about Amelia Bedelia:

1. She's *very* funny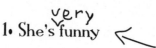

2. She's brave

3. She's a good friend ♥

4. She loves to read

5. She'll try anything

6. She makes really good cookies

7. She takes things literally

8. She never gives up

9. She loves her family

10. She always helps out

# If you were going to explore the world, where would you go?

Amelia Bedelia dreams of exploring . . .

- The Great Sphinx in Egypt

- The Mayan pyramids in Central America

- The rain forest

- The streets of Rome